The Capture

Nancy Rue

BETHANY HOUSE PUBLISHERS
MINNEAPOLIS, MINNESOTA 55438

The Capture
Copyright © 1999
Nancy N. Rue

Cover illustration by Cheri Bladholm
Cover design by Bradley Lind

This author is represented by the literary agency of Alive Communications,
1465 Kelly Johnson Blvd., Suite 320, Colorado Springs, CO 80920.

This story is a work of fiction. All characters are the product of the author's
imagination. Any resemblance to any person, living or dead, is coincidental.

A Focus on the Family book
Published by Bethany House Publishers
A Ministry of Bethany Fellowship International
11400 Hampshire Avenue South
Minneapolis, Minnesota 55438
www.bethanyhouse.com

Printed in the United States of America by
Bethany Press International, Minneapolis, Minnesota 55438

Library of Congress Cataloging-in-Publication Data

Rue, Nancy N.
    The capture / Nancy Rue.
       p.   cm. — (Christian heritage series. The Chicago years ; 3)
    Summary: For ten-year-old Rudy, Christmastime in Chicago in 1928
brings a school pageant, his father's court case about a Jewish boy accused of
a shooting that may involve mobsters, and a kidnapping.
    ISBN 1–56179–810–X
    [1. Chicago (Ill.) Fiction. 2. Gangsters Fiction. 3. Christmas Fiction.
4. Jews—United States Fiction. 5. Christian life Fiction.] I. Title.
II. Series: Rue, Nancy N. Christian heritage series. Chicago years ; 3.
PZ7.R88515Cap 1999
[Fic]—DC21
                                            99–27161
                                              CIP

99 00 01 02 03 04 05 / 15 14 13 12 11 10 9 8 7 6 5 4 3 2 1

For Robin Wolf,
whose gentle care and faithful prayers
helped me write
The Capture

Chapter One

*R*udolph Hutchinson, you touch that cookie and so help me you'll draw you back a nub!"

Though he really preferred to be called "Rudy," 10-year-old Rudolph Hutchinson pulled his hand away from the pan full of star-shaped sugar cookies and grinned up at Quintonia. She didn't grin back.

"Don't you be makin' up no story 'bout how you was just keepin' a eye on 'em for me, neither," Quintonia said. She wiped her hands on her housemaid's apron and glared at Rudy. He continued to grin.

"Give up, Quintonia," Rudy's twin sister, Hildy Helen, said. "He isn't afraid of you anymore."

"I never was," Rudy said. To prove it, he reached for the cookie sheet again. Quintonia popped his hand lightly with a spatula.

"I was, and still am," Little Al said. He pulled his tight little mouth into a half smile at Quintonia. "But then, I like a tough doll like you."

"I ain't no doll, Alonzo Delgado," Quintonia said. "And don't you be forgettin' that."

But this time she did smile, and so did Rudy as he shook his head. His adopted brother could charm just about anybody.

1

"Now, I've fed you children a good lunch," Quintonia said, trying to replace her smile with a stern look. "Almost time for you to head back to school. I'd guess you can make it through the afternoon without eating a bunch of cookies."

"I still think you should let us test them," Hildy Helen said. She tucked her thick bob of dark hair behind her ears. "We won't get germs on them or anything."

"We could make sure they're all right to eat," Rudy put in.

"And why wouldn't they be?" Quintonia said, eyebrows shooting up her dark forehead.

"You never can tell," Little Al said. "Al Capone, he has his chef test everything 'fore he eats it—just in case somebody's poisoned his food."

"Who in the world's gonna poison our food?" Quintonia said. She gave a disgusted hiss and removed the cookie sheet from Rudy's reach. "Go on and get out of here, all three of you. I can't be standin' around jawin' 'bout gangsters. I got to get some serious bakin' done. December's here, and you know what that means."

"But the Christmas Eve party is weeks away," Hildy Helen said. "These cookies will be stale by then."

"Small chance of that, with the appetites in this house," said a voice from the doorway.

Rudy jumped. It didn't matter that he'd lived in this house for six months now. Whenever his great-aunt Gussie entered a room unexpectedly, he still jumped. She just did that to people. He made sure he wasn't anywhere near Quintonia's cookies.

"Perhaps this baking project is research for the upcoming Christmas rush," Aunt Gussie said. "Not that Quintonia needs the practice, of course." She swept into the kitchen, sensible pumps tapping the gleaming floor, gray hair shimmering in waves under the bright light of the electric bulbs. The whole kitchen seemed to try to look its shiniest when Aunt Gussie was in it.

"It's exciting," Hildy Helen said. "Dad never made this much of a fuss over Christmas back in Shelbyville."

Rudy had to agree with her there. They'd grown up without a mother; she had died when they were small. And their attorney father had always buried his head in his law books and cases until about two days before Christmas, when he would look up vaguely and say, "Oh, is it that time of year again?"

But not Aunt Gussie. Ever since Thanksgiving there had been nothing but Christmas preparations going on inside the big old house on Prairie Avenue.

Quintonia was shopping for everything from roast beef to raisins, getting ready for Aunt Gussie's annual Christmas Eve open house. Sol, her ancient chauffeur, was dragging the decorations out of the attic and climbing ladders to hang wreaths and string garlands. Aunt Gussie was on the phone arranging Christmas events for the many charities she managed. Bridget, Aunt Gussie's live-in secretary, was writing invitations and addressing Christmas cards. And the twins and Little Al, of course, were poking their noses into all of it.

It was hard not to. Everything was being decorated, right down to Picasso the parrot's cage in the library. The whole place was starting to smell of cinnamon and nutmeg and peppermint, and the strains of Little Al practicing carols on his violin wafted out of the music room every afternoon.

And that was just at the house. Christmas, the twins discovered, involved every inch of the whole city of Chicago, too. There was the *Nutcracker* ballet at the Fine Arts Institute, and *Amahl and the Night Visitors* at the Civic Opera House. And of course there was the special Rosetti exhibit at the Art Institute of Chicago—to which Aunt Gussie had taken Rudy alone so they could linger in front of the paintings as long as they wanted to without Hildy Helen and Little Al sighing loudly in the background. For Aunt Gussie, the program at Hull House was the best part of Christmas. Each nationality at Jane Addams's settlement house did a nativity scene in its country's tradition.

The one thing all of them loved was the shopping. Last Saturday Aunt Gussie had piled the kids and Bridget into the Pierce Arrow and Sol had driven them downtown, where the city sparkled with red and green and everything Christmas. Storefronts blazed with decorations—the clothes shops, the candy stores, even the drug stores.

Marshall Field's department store, the one with the big clocks on the corner of State Street, was Hildy Helen's favorite. Though she gazed for what seemed like hours at the displays of long strings of beads and gauzy chemise dresses, she also hinted at a burning desire for a Raggedy Ann doll. It didn't matter that she was nearly 12. It was their first real Christmas.

Little Al, on the other hand, eyed the belted cashmere jackets—while Aunt Gussie eyed their eight-dollar price tag. She had more money than anybody Rudy had ever known, but she still muttered, "Highway robbery!" as she hustled them all past the store windows.

"Come on, Miss Gustavio," Little Al said to her, "you oughta be glad I ain't got the eye for them Russian sable coats." He whistled into the glass at the furrier's. "Fifty grand!"

"I could feed several nations with that kind of money," Aunt Gussie told him. Then glancing at Little Al who was Italian and Bridget who was Irish, she said, "In fact, I already am."

Rudy just liked the hustle and bustle of Christmas in the city. There were over three million people in Chicago, and every one of them seemed to crowd onto the icy sidewalks and puff out frosty air on those Saturday afternoons—and all with a delicious anticipation. It didn't matter that he got jostled by overcoat-clad elbows while picking out a crossword puzzle book for Dad or was stepped on by galoshes while watching an old man roast chestnuts on the curb. As far as he was concerned, it was all part of the fun. When they would go to the grand Stephens Hotel on Michigan Avenue for dessert after shopping, Rudy would start right in drawing cartoon caricatures of the people he'd seen. He was doing a whole Christmas collection.

"Did you remember that I asked for a wind-up Victrola of my own?" Hildy Helen was saying now. "Then I could listen to Rudy Vallee all I wanted instead of waiting for the Fleischmann Hour on the radio."

Rudy looked at Aunt Gussie in time to see her lips pursing and her small eyes narrowing behind her glasses. "Not much chance of me forgetting that, either," she said.

"Yeah," said Little Al, "but how much chance is there of her actually gettin' it?" He winked at Rudy.

"I hope she does forget," Rudy said. "I hate the way that fella sings through his nose with that hokey megaphone."

"You're just jealous because you're not the most famous Rudy in the world." That came from Bridget McBrien, who sailed in with her knee-length chemise flowing around her, and her curly, bobbed, red hair flowing around her face. "Got any hot cocoa, Quintonia?"

"Hot cocoa?" Quintonia said.

"Ooh, that does sound good!" Hildy Helen said. "Hot cocoa is my favorite! I could drink it eight times a day."

Aunt Gussie nodded at Quintonia, who protested. "It ain't like I don't already got enough to do, gettin' ready for this party."

"It's not so much, Quintonia," Aunt Gussie said. "We don't entertain like we used to, before the war. Now you have to admit that. You make the cocoa and I'll set out the cups."

Quintonia was admitting nothing. She grumbled to herself as she reached for the can of cocoa.

"Back to my wardrobe," Little Al said. He sidled up to Bridget. "What was that you was tellin' me—you know, about the well-dressed businessman?"

"I read it in a magazine," Bridget said. "The well-dressed businessman should have 20 suits, 12 hats, 8 overcoats, and 24 pairs of shoes."

"That is the most ridiculous thing I have ever heard!" Aunt Gussie said. "Do you know how many countries I could clothe for the amount of money it would take to purchase all those things for one boy?"

"I'm Italian, so that could count as one country," Little Al said brightly. He was the one person who had never been afraid of Aunt Gussie.

"I shouldn't be surprised you're all so materialistic," Aunt Gussie said as she opened a glass-doored cabinet to pull out cups. "Our whole society has become money hungry. That's all anybody can seem to think about."

"I don't want money," Little Al said. "I just want some of them pants that hang over yer heels. Gray flannel. I seen 'em in the Sears catalog."

"They're called Oxford bags," Bridget said. Her eyes sparkled at the kids. They all knew what was coming.

"That is precisely what I'm talking about!" Aunt Gussie said. "Once again you have proven my point, Alonzo. And you will not wear pants that look three sizes too big. They are incredibly unbecoming."

"Aw, come on, Miss Gustavio," Little Al said. "Hey, have I told you I like an old doll like you?"

Aunt Gussie ignored that and went on plunking cups onto the table. Quintonia watched her warily out of the corner of her eye. She protected the kitchenware with her life.

"Now remember, Aunt Gussie," Hildy Helen said. "I want a Victrola with a lid cover—oh, and a bamboo needle. Those are the best."

"Do you children think my money grows on trees?" Aunt Gussie said.

"No," Hildy Helen said. "But I heard on the radio that President Hoover is promising four more years of prosperity. Doesn't that mean everybody will have enough money?"

"That's what it means, but it's a lie."

Rudy wriggled on the kitchen chair. He hated it when his aunt started talking about politics and stuff. She was always going on about how people were foolish to put all their extra money into the stock market and, worse, borrow money to buy stocks so they would get even richer. What it had to do with him, he could never figure out.

"People are buying everything on credit," Aunt Gussie said. "When it all comes crashing down, they'll be sorry. They'll be worse than sorry. They'll be broke."

"I thought you said money wasn't that important," Hildy Helen said.

"Being rich isn't important," Aunt Gussie said. "But being able to survive, now that is. And so is you getting yourselves back to school." She nodded toward the steaming cups of cocoa Quintonia was filling from the double boiler. "Drink up and get going. You'll be late."

Lunchtime seems to be going by faster than ever these days, Rudy thought. Probably because there was so much going on here at the house. He'd just as soon not go back just to practice the dumb old Christmas program.

But that wasn't true for Hildy Helen. She winced as she took a hot gulp of cocoa and looked up at the clock. She never wanted to miss a minute of rehearsal. She was the lead dancer. The lead "hoofer," Little Al called her. And he was nearly as excited about the rehearsals as Hildy Helen was. Miss Tibbs, their teacher, had placed him on the front row and given him a big speaking part, and Al loved nothing better than to be the center of attention. He told Rudy when they were measured for their silky costume pants—which Rudy wouldn't have been caught dead in if Miss

Tibbs weren't making him wear them—that he'd found a way to have his made like the baggy pants he dreamed of.

Al blew the steam off his cup and gave Quintonia a half smile. "Now don't forget," Al said to her. "Yer gonna try makin' some cannoli this afternoon—to practice for Christmas Eve."

"I know," Quintonia said. "It ain't enough I got to make six punkin and mincemeat pies—and more cookies than you can shake a stick at. Now I got to act like some Eye-talian cook in my own kitchen."

"You got the cream cheese?" Little Al said. "The pistachio nuts?"

Bridget laughed her silvery little laugh. "Don't start whining, Quintonia," she said. "You know you love it."

Quintonia grunted. They all knew she liked doing things for them, but they weren't going to get that information out of *her*. Besides, Aunt Gussie was now bent on ushering them all out the door and back to school.

"I'd rather stay here," Rudy said. "It's more fun."

"Fine," Aunt Gussie said, handing him his muffler. "I was going to polish the silver punch bowl. You can do that for me."

Rudy grabbed the muffler and tossed it around his neck.

"I thought so," she said. "And just in case you get bored this afternoon, here's something I want all of you to think about."

"Uh-oh," Hildy Helen said into her wool scarf.

"I'm more than a little concerned about your attitudes about Christmas, all of you," she said. "I think I've put too much emphasis on the shopping and the gift-giving and not enough on the true meaning."

"Jesus was born in a manger, just like a regular guy," Little Al said. "See, Miss Gustavio? We got it."

"We'll see," Aunt Gussie said. "I've decided each of you must give to the others a gift from the heart—something Jesus would be proud to have you give." She paused to let that sink in. "And," she added, "it cannot cost a dime."

"How are we supposed to know what Jesus would be proud of?" Hildy Helen asked as they headed off down Prairie Avenue toward Felthensal School.

Little Al shrugged and started describing a shiny silver yo-yo, which he was also hoping to find in his Christmas stocking. Rudy, however, knew exactly what he was going to do.

I've got a gift, he mused to himself. Aunt Gussie herself had told him his passion for art and for the people he drew came from God. *Anything I draw'll be somethin' Jesus would like, so what have I got to worry about?*

As he trudged on through the gray slush behind Hildy Helen and Little Al, his glasses fogging up in the cold, he had to admit he really didn't worry about much of anything these days—not since he'd started doing more drawings of Jesus. That was one of the ways he prayed—drawing his ideas of what Jesus looked like and what He would say to do in a certain situation. *I've got being a Christian wrapped up*, Rudy told himself. *That's why everything's going so well.*

No sooner had he thought that than they arrived in the school yard. And who should leap in front of them, seemingly out of nowhere, but Maury Worthington. Rudy felt himself frowning. Things never went well when Maury's face was on the scene. Right now it was bright red from the cold, and the way the frost was puffing out of his nose, he looked like a nearly frozen bull.

"Out of our way, Worthington," Little Al said. "We gotta get to play practice."

"Yeah, well, that's why I'm here," Maury said. From the way his teeth were chattering and his nostrils were dripping, he'd been "here" for quite some time waiting for them. He hunched his bulky shoulders up against the frigid air. "I got somethin' to say about this Christmas pageant thing."

"Can't you say it inside?" Hildy Helen said. "It's freezing out here. My muscles are going to get all stiff, and I won't be able to dance."

"Too bad," Maury said. "You shouldn't be dancin' anyhow—at least not as the main dancer."

"Here we go again," Little Al said.

Rudy shook his head, causing his dark curls to spill out from under his cap and onto his forehead. "Forget it, Maury," he said. "Miss Tibbs picked Hildy Helen to be the lead dancer—not Dorothea."

"Huh," Maury said. "Shows how much that dame knows about dancin'. My sister's been takin' lessons since she was four." He jerked his reddening nose at Hildy Helen. "How long you been takin'? Three months?"

"Funny how she's 20 times better'n yer sister with only a coupla lessons," Little Al said. "Ever heard of a thing called 'talent?' "

The warning bell clanged from inside the school, and Rudy poked his mittened hands into Little Al and Hildy Helen's backs. "Come on, we're gonna be late."

Maury grunted as he watched the three of them go by. "Yer sure a goody-goody now," he said to Rudy. "You think you got a halo or somethin'?"

Rudy ignored him as they hurried into the building and up to Miss Tibbs's sixth-grade classroom on the second floor. Maury was right about one thing—Rudy didn't get into as much trouble for being the class clown as he used to. But he sure didn't think he was a goody-goody.

I still know a million jokes I could play on you, Maury, Rudy thought as he hung up his coat in the cloakroom. *If I wanted to*.

But things were going so well, what with Christmas coming and all, why should he want to? Even a bully like Maury Worthington and his whiny little sister would have to do something pretty bad before Rudy would pull a joke and ruin his current perfect record.

And then, wouldn't you know it? The Worthingtons did.

✠ ⬥ ✠

Chapter Two

*W*hen the whole sixth-grade class was in place on the stage in the assembly hall, Miss Tibbs silently raised her hand to get their attention. Miss Tibbs never screamed at the top of her lungs the way Rudy had heard some other teachers do. He had to admit he liked that about her—that and a few other things. But she was still, in fact, a teacher. He and Hildy Helen had always agreed that it was best not to get too chummy with the person who had the power to get you into big trouble with your father.

"All right, class," she said, her green-flecked-with-gold eyes shining at them. "We have only a few more rehearsals, so let's make the most of our time. Now—"

"Miss Tibbs!"

Rudy craned his neck from the second row of risers to see that Maury, standing in the front row near Al, had shot his thick arm up into the air.

"What is it, Maury?" Miss Tibbs said.

"I gotta be on the end."

"Why?"

"I don't feel so good. I might have to go upchuck really fast. I'd hate to throw up all over—"

Miss Tibbs held up her hand. "Fine, Maury," she said. "And

from now on, be careful what you eat for lunch, would you?"

He probably ate a whole cow or something, Rudy thought, watching Maury move to the end of the row, right next to Al.

Miss Tibbs ran a hand over her sandy blonde waves as she watched the rearrangement. "All right, boys. Am I taking a chance putting you two side by side?" she said. Her mouth was good-humored as always, but Rudy knew she meant business. So, evidently, did Little Al.

"Not on yer life, Miss Dollface," he said. "I plan on keepin' him in line."

Maury's pale face went scarlet. "Says you!"

"No one is going to 'say' anything," Miss Tibbs said mildly. "Miss Erwin, let's begin, shall we, before I have another war on my hands?"

Miss Erwin, the teacher at the piano, pulled in her lips until they looked like one big prune and started the music. Most of the other teachers in the school thought Miss Tibbs was too "progressive" in her teaching philosophy. That's what Rudy had heard her tell his father on one of the many occasions she'd visited their house. Hildy Helen had explained that meant she didn't slap enough wrists with rulers and that kind of thing.

"Pay attention!" Miss Tibbs whispered to them.

Rudy tried not to look too utterly bored as Miss Erwin plunked at the keys and Little Al started reciting his lines over the noise. Rudy was pretty sure Miss Tibbs had picked him for the part because he had the best set of lungs in the class. It must've been from growing up shouting in the streets of the West Side's Little Italy.

It was time for the chorus to start humming, and although he felt like a goof doing it, Rudy joined in. He kept his eye out for Hildy Helen, who any second now was going to enter from the left wing leading a string of dancers that, in his opinion, couldn't begin to keep up with her hoofing.

Hildy Helen did indeed enter, wearing a dazzling smile and holding her hands out gracefully as she floated across the stage like a snowflake. Rudy thought the whole idea was pretty goofy, but Hildy Helen managed to be convincing.

Little Al's right, he thought. *She's 10 times better than Dorothea, even with only a couple months of lessons.*

Pale Dorothea Worthington followed Hildy Helen onstage, attempting the snowflake attitude with her long, thin arms.

She's a snowflake, all right, Rudy thought. *She's a half-melted one!*

It was a shame about Dorothea, really. She had such an overbite to her wide mouth, it allowed her hook nose to dip almost to her chin, which scooped up to meet it. Between that and the way she squinted out ahead of her because she needed glasses and refused to wear them, she was a pathetic sight even when she wasn't dancing. Add steps and arm motions to her, and she was pitiful—and looked even more so behind sure-footed Hildy Helen.

Rudy stifled a snort. *And Maury thinks* she *oughta be the lead dancer? Bushwa!*

The dancers reached the edge of the risers, and Rudy craned his neck farther to see Hildy Helen twirl. She was forever practicing her twirl—on the sidewalk on the way to school, in the upstairs hall while she was waiting for somebody to get out of the bathroom. When Aunt Gussie saw her twirling down the stairs, she said it was a wonder Hildy Helen didn't break her neck.

"Watch me!" Miss Tibbs hissed to the singers.

Rudy riveted his eyes on her. He could see Hildy Helen twirl anytime, anywhere. No sense getting Miss Tibbs on his back right before vacation.

"Hey!" somebody suddenly shrieked. The only person who could squall like that was Dorothea Worthington. Everybody craned toward the dancers, and Miss Tibbs waved for Miss Erwin to stop plunking.

"What on earth?" Miss Tibbs said. "Hildy Helen, what's wrong?"

Rudy didn't wait for his sister to answer. He shoved Earl and Fox out of the way and jumped to the stage floor. Miss Tibbs was just squatting down beside Hildy Helen, who was sprawled out looking nothing like a snowflake.

"What happened?" Miss Tibbs said.

"Something got in my way," Hildy Helen said. "One minute I was twirling, and the next minute I was down here."

"She must have tripped over her own foot," Dorothea said. Her nose nearly met her chin in a twisted smile. "That used to happen to me all the time when I was a beginner."

Rudy opened his mouth to set her straight, but a moan from Hildy Helen stopped him.

"Where does it hurt?" Miss Tibbs said.

"My ankle," Hildy Helen said. "I can't put any weight on it."

"Probably broken," Maury said, shaking his big head.

Little Al scowled up at him. "Since when was you a doctor?" he said. "Hildy Helen's a tough little doll. She's all right."

But from the way Hildy Helen's face contorted when she tried to stand up, Rudy knew she was anything but all right. She leaned heavily on Miss Tibbs, and her big brown eyes filled up with tears. She bit her lip, though. The Hutchinson kids didn't cry in front of other people—especially not the Worthingtons.

And particularly not Dorothea, who was trying to cover a smile with her hand as she shook her head.

Huh! Rudy thought angrily. *I bet she tripped Hildy herself!*

Once again Rudy started to say so, but Miss Tibbs cut in. "I'm going to take Hildy Helen down to the infirmary. Miss Erwin, go ahead with the music. Dorothea, can you fill in for Hildy for today?"

"I'll do it for as long as you want," Dorothea said. This time, she couldn't hide the triumphant smile.

Rudy really wanted to slug her, and he could tell Little Al was itching to as well. It was the longest rehearsal yet, and the minute they were released that afternoon, they both bolted for the infirmary with steam practically coming out of their ears.

"I'd like to tell her a thing or two," Rudy said through his teeth as the two boys hurried down the stairs.

"Who?" Little Al said.

"Dorothea, who else?"

"Why her? It was Maury that done it. I seen him stick his foot right out there."

Rudy didn't ask why Little Al hadn't spoken up to Miss Tibbs. He knew Al liked to take matters into his own hands. "What are you planning?" Rudy said.

"Nothin' but all-out war on both of 'em—and George and Clark and Victor and the rest of their gang."

"I don't know—" Rudy began. His stomach churned uneasily.

"Whattya mean, ya don't know? We gotta stick up for Hildy Helen—"

"Yeah, but we can't be sluggin' people out on the playground."

Little Al frowned. "I keep forgettin' I gotta keep my nose clean now." He pulled the back of his hand under the nose in question and sniffed. "Just for a minute I'd like to be a hood again, y'know?"

"Yeah, I know," Rudy said. "Sometimes I hate bein' a goody-goody."

He reached out to turn the handle of the door marked INFIRMARY, but Little Al grabbed his wrist.

"Hey, Rudolpho!" he said. "I got an idea!"

"Yeah?"

"You ain't played a joke on nobody in a long time."

"Yeah, and I haven't got in trouble in a long time, either."

"So who says you gotta get in trouble?"

"I always do!"

Little Al shrugged and followed Rudy into the nurse's office. Hildy Helen was lying on a cot, ankle propped up on two pillows and face in a scowl. The tears were gone, and in their place were sparks.

"It was Maury who did this, huh?" she said to Little Al.

"Yeah. I was watchin' Miss Tibbs, but I seen him out of the corner of my eye. I got a sense for that kinda thing, if ya know what I mean."

"So, what are we going to do about it?" Hildy Helen said.

Little Al shrugged again, looking elaborately up at the ceiling.

"What do you mean you don't know? We're going to do *something*, aren't we?" Hildy Helen demanded.

"Rudy says we gotta keep our noses clean," Little Al said. He gave an exaggerated sigh. "I figure he knows best—"

"Applesauce!" Hildy Helen cried. "Rudy Hutchinson, if it was *you* who'd been tripped to fall on your face in front of everybody, you can bet I'd get even!"

"By doing what?" Rudy said miserably. "Anything we do is gonna get us in trouble."

"I told him he should play a joke on Maury—y'know, somethin' nobody would ever find out about because Maury'd be too embarrassed to tell."

"Of course," Hildy Helen said. "Rudy, there was a time when you'd have thought of a dozen things already."

"I have," Rudy said, tilting up his chin.

"Well?"

Rudy looked at both of them. They were watching him, eyes wide, every muscle tensed for action—except that Hildy Helen *couldn't* be part of the action because her ankle was swelling up like a sausage and turning purple right before his eyes.

"All right," he said. "But it's gotta be done quiet-like."

"No problem!" Little Al exclaimed. "I can be quiet!"

"Then how about doing it?" A white cap poked around the doorway from the inner office, and the school nurse put her finger to her lips. "I've called your house to send someone to pick up Hildegarde," she said in a voice as starched as her uniform. "Why don't you two go outside and wait? You're getting her all stirred up."

"I was just thinkin' that myself," Little Al said. He ran a hand smoothly over his slicked-back dark hair and gave the nurse one of his charmer smiles. She smiled back, and the cap disappeared.

"Go! Scram!" Hildy Helen whispered to the boys. "I'll see you at home. And you'd better tell me every single thing that happens."

"Every detail," Little Al said. "Don't worry about nothin'."

Hildy Helen was smiling when they left, and that alone spurred Rudy on out to the playground. He did look over his shoulder several times to make sure nobody was watching from a window, but Little Al nudged him with his elbow.

"Don't you worry 'bout nothin', Rudolpho," he said. "We're aces at this kinda stuff."

"Don't I know it!" Rudy said. He felt his face sliding into a grin. This really wasn't going to hurt anybody. And Maury had it coming. He couldn't just let him get away with this.

"Psst! There he is!" Little Al said in a hoarse whisper.

Rudy followed his gaze to the other side of the pointed iron fence, where Maury sat on the top of an empty metal bike rack. His three constant companions, George, Victor, and Clark, stood in front of him, picking their noses as usual.

"What do you want me to do, boss?" Little Al said, his eyes gleaming with anticipation.

"You get the three wise guys' attention away from Maury," Rudy said. "Leave the rest to me."

"This is gonna be sweet," Al said.

Then he seemed to rise right up off the sidewalk, and Rudy had to peer upward to see that he'd just shinnied up an oak tree. The branches were winter-naked, but Al was already climbing high enough to escape the notice of the casual passer-by. Rudy snickered to himself and waited behind the tree trunk. What Little Al would do to distract them was anybody's guess.

Rudy didn't have to wait long to find out. Like a missile in a Tom Swift novel, a rock suddenly flew from the tree and smacked Maury Worthington square in the back of his jacket. He whirled around to look, his thick face ruddy with the cold.

"Who done that?" Maury said.

His three cohorts all pointed in the vague general direction of the oak tree. Rudy didn't dare peek out any longer. He flattened himself against the bark and listened as Maury ordered George, Victor, and Clark to go investigate. He heard one of them yelp as they approached, and he knew Al had fired another projectile at them. Just as Rudy figured they were about at the fence, he heard a thud and a series of yells. Little Al had made his entrance and was obviously leading them on a chase to the other side of the playground. Rudy peeled himself away from the tree and vaulted the pointy-topped fence. Maury sat on the bike rack, peering after his chums but not moving an inch to help them.

Some friend, Rudy thought. *I'm not like that. I'm glad now that I didn't just let this go.*

Shoulders squared, he strolled on over to Maury. "Hey," he said. "Where'd everybody go?"

Maury jumped, nearly tumbling off the bike rack. Rudy bit back a laugh.

"What do you mean, sneakin' up on me, goof?" Maury said.

"Sorry," Rudy said. He let his face go into an innocent blank. "I just wondered why everybody left you by yourself. Maybe you forgot to take a bath this week?"

Maury glared at him so hard, his eyebrows almost covered his eyes. "Yeah, I took a bath! What's it to you?"

"Nothin'," Rudy said. Then he stared across the playground, where Little Al and Maury's cohorts had gone. "Maybe you oughta go check to see where they went."

"Why?" Maury said. "What do you want me to leave for?"

"No reason," said Rudy.

"You got some kinda secret or somethin'?"

Rudy slapped his hand over his mouth and rolled his eyes. "Drat," he mumbled.

"You do!" Maury said. He managed to get his big self off the bike rack, and he stood over Rudy. As always, the sight of Maury's almost babyish face on that huge, lumbering body made Rudy want to burst out laughing—and then run for the nearest sketch pad to get it down again. But Rudy controlled himself and went on with his act.

"I can't get anything past you, can I, Maury?" he said.

"No," Maury said, drawing himself up even taller. "I been tryin' to tell you that ever since you moved here. I'm the richest kid here, and Dorothea's the smartest. The sooner you and yer sister and yer 'brother' get that into your heads, the happier everybody's gonna be."

Rudy scratched his cap with his mittened hand. "I think I'm gettin' it. Maybe I oughta just tell you the secret instead of tryin' to pull it over on ya."

"Yeah," Maury said. His eyes warmed with interest. "I think maybe you oughta."

Rudy made a big show of swallowing hard, and then he pointed to the metal uprights on the bike rack. Maury looked and blinked.

"What?" he said. "Ain't nobody parked a bike here for two years. Not since me and the boys took it over as our sittin' place."

"Nobody's gonna mess with you and the boys, that's for sure," Rudy said. "I thought maybe I'd get out here when you weren't here, but it looks like I underestimated you."

"Don't be usin' them big words," Maury said. His mouth went into a heavy frown. "Just come out with it."

"Oh, I forgot," Rudy said. "It's your sister that's the smart one. You're the rich one."

"And the tough one, so spit it out!"

"All right, all right. I was just comin' out here to see if what they say about the bike rack is true."

"See if what's true?"

"That it gets so frosty in winter, lickin' it is like eatin' an Epicle down at the pier in the summer."

Maury looked at the bike rack, his heavy lower lip now hanging as if its hinge had come loose. Rudy watched him inspect the hairy-looking frost that had collected on the metal. Maury's mouth pulled slowly into a grin.

"It does kinda look like ice cream, don't it?"

"That's what I thought!" Rudy said. "So I asked around and sure enough, they say it even tastes like it. Only—"

"Only what?" Maury said, losing the grin.

"Only everybody kinda figures this thing is yours and nobody wants to take a chance on licking it and getting caught by you."

"Including you?" Maury said. His eyes took on a pleased gleam. It was all Rudy could do not to bust out laughing.

"Especially me!" Rudy said. He adjusted his glasses with visibly shaking fingers. "I've been beat up by you enough times. That's why I was hoping you wouldn't be around."

"Well, I am," Maury said. "And all of a sudden, you're not, if you get what I mean."

Rudy pretended to be stumped for a minute and then made a huge "oh" with his lips. "I get what you mean," he said. He whirled on his heel and headed for the fence. "I think I'll just be goin' now."

"I think you will," Maury said.

Rudy heard him chuckling, and he forced himself not to turn around and watch until he was over the fence. When he did, Maury was just leaning down to place his tongue against the frosted metal.

That's it, Maury, Rudy thought gleefully. *Now take a big slurp!*

Maury did, and then he froze. From his open mouth came a whimper—which turned into a holler as he tried in vain to pull his tongue from the metal.

Rudy stuffed his hand, mitten and all, into his mouth to smother his delight as he took off down the sidewalk and left Maury Worthington with his tongue stuck to the bike rack. Rudy knew Hildy Helen was going to love this, and he couldn't wait to tell her.

✢ ✢ ✢

Chapter Three

*R*udy didn't get a chance to tell Hildy Helen at first. He had gotten home later than usual, and Quintonia already had supper on the table. Aunt Gussie met him at the door and told him to get washed up because they had company.

"Who is it?" Rudy said. He hoped it was Judge Caduff, the former boxer friend of his father's who always made things interesting at the table.

"Colonel Robert McCormick, if you must know," Aunt Gussie said.

"Who's Colonel Robert McCormick?"

"Get those hands washed so you can come down and find out for yourself," Aunt Gussie said. "And hurry. Everyone else is already at the table."

Rudy was still drying his palms on the backs of his knickers when he got to the dining room. *Colonel McCormick must be somebody important*, Rudy thought, because there were candles glowing in the bronze candlesticks—the ones with the claw feet Aunt Gussie had brought over from Italy on one of her many trips. The house was fairly bursting with strange artifacts, but these she brought out only for special occasions.

Rudy slipped into place next to Little Al and only glanced

briefly across the table at a large man with fierce eyes. Rudy focused on Hildy Helen's empty chair.

"Where's Hildy?" he said.

"She's having her supper in her room," Aunt Gussie said. "She needs to stay off that ankle, and if it isn't better by morning I'm calling Dr. Netzer."

"It'll be better," Little Al said. "Hildy Helen's one tough little doll."

"So you've said," Bridget said dryly.

"Now if you've finished inquiring as to everyone's whereabouts, Rudy," Aunt Gussie said, "I'll introduce you to Colonel McCormick. Robert, this is my nephew Rudolph. Rudolph, Colonel McCormick of the *Chicago Tribune*."

"Call me Rudy," Rudy said as he nodded at the man. "So you're a reporter, huh?"

"Not quite. He's the editor of the *Tribune*." It was the first time Rudy's father had spoken since Rudy had come into the dining room. That wasn't unusual. Dad was a hardworking lawyer. He almost always had something else on his mind other than what was going on in the room around him. Until recently, it had been easy to get things by him because of that—but these days, between Miss Tibbs and Aunt Gussie, Dad was picking up a lot more. That had its good and bad points.

"Editor! Hot dog!" Little Al said. He gave an impressed whistle.

For the first time, the man smiled. "It's not so much as you might think," he said.

"Of course it is, Robert," Aunt Gussie said. "Don't sell yourself short. As soon as we've said the blessing, I want you to tell the boys just how influential you are. It might show them how important their studies are if they want to be men of your importance."

Rudy tried to pay attention to the blessing—after all, he and

Jesus were pals now—but as soon as it was over, he went after his chicken potpie and hoped somebody would change the subject. Every time Aunt Gussie wanted to teach them a lesson about something, the conversation got deadly boring.

"I wouldn't say I was all that influential, Gussie," Robert McCormick said. "Not after this last trip to Washington."

"What happened?" Dad said. "Were you able to speak with the president?"

"President-elect," McCormick said. "No use talking to Calvin Coolidge now, not that there ever was."

"Is Herbert Hoover going to be any better?" Aunt Gussie said.

Rudy squirmed. He really hated talking about politics.

"You can judge for yourself," McCormick said. "I finally got a meeting with him—20 minutes was all he could spare, so I gave him a short rundown on the crime situation here in Chicago. He said to me, 'What about the Department of Justice? Why don't you go to them?' I said, 'The Department of Justice isn't even touching Al Capone.'" McCormick groaned. "And you know what he said to me then?"

"What?" said Bridget. She'd stopped eating her pot pie and was leaning forward, fork suspended in midair.

"He said, 'Who's Al Capone?'"

Aunt Gussie gasped. "Say it isn't so!"

"Wish I could, Gussie."

"You set him straight, didn't ya, mister?" Little Al said. "Everybody knows who Al Capone is!"

"He does now," McCormick said. "What he's going to do about it remains to be seen. Then we'll see just how influential I really am."

"You can't discount what you've done for the readers of the *Tribune*," Aunt Gussie said. "You've educated them. You haven't pandered to their thirst for the sensational like the other papers."

"Colonel McCormick," Bridget said, still pressing against the table in fascination, "is it true that you've walked the streets of Chicago disguised as a blind man just to get a scoop? Would you tell us?"

He probably would have, and the evening would have turned out to be far better than it did—but the doorbell rang, and everyone lapsed into small talk while Quintonia hurried to get it. When she returned to the dining room, she had another guest behind her. Rudy felt his eyes pop. It was Miss Tibbs.

"Effa Mae, I didn't know if you'd make it or not, so we started without you," Aunt Gussie said. "Please forgive us."

"Don't give it a thought, Gustavia," Miss Tibbs said. "Something came up at school at the last minute."

Her green-gold eyes swept the table and came to a stop right on Rudy. Something in them turned his salad to rubber in his mouth. One thing was obvious: "Something" was connected to him, and he was going to hear about it before the night was over.

The conversation turned to the state of things in Europe, where, the colonel declared, things were in such chaos, it was no wonder everyone in the United States was afraid of what might happen.

"Of course we're afraid of being oppressed!" Bridget said.

"Then stay informed," the colonel told her with a wink. "Read the *Tribune*."

Then the grown-ups talked about something called the Old Order being destroyed. But all Rudy could think about was wolfing down his chicken potpie, passing up the pie à la mode, and getting away from that table before Miss Tibbs had the chance to point the finger at him.

"May I be excused, please?" he said, mouth still stuffed with pastry and chicken gravy. "I want to check on Hildy Helen."

"Yes, please go," Aunt Gussie said, "before your manners embarrass me to death."

"Boys have other things to think about, eh, Jim?" the colonel said to Dad.

"Now, what about this Chicago crime commission?" Dad said.

Good, Rudy thought as he slipped out of the dining room, with Little Al not far behind him. *He's too wrapped up in that colonel fella to pay any attention to what Miss Tibbs has on her mind.*

Little Al and Rudy entertained Hildy Helen with their versions of Maury and the frozen tongue. Then they went to the head of the stairs to make sure Dad was still being held under the colonel's spell, and they heard Aunt Gussie say, "I'm sorry you have to leave so early, Robert. You're outlandish, but I delight in your company."

"The news doesn't stand still while I'm at a dinner party, Gussie," the colonel said, and to Rudy's dismay, he headed for the front door.

"Where's Miss Dollface?" Little Al whispered as they peered down from the stair landing. "And Mr. Hutchie?"

"I hope you'll excuse James's lack of social graces," Aunt Gussie said from the front door. "He was down in Indiana too long, I'm afraid."

"Nothing more important than his children's education," the colonel said. "And with a teacher like that, I'd be shut up in the library with her, too!"

"You are impossible!" Aunt Gussie said, and then she laughed, not something one heard from her often.

But Rudy wasn't laughing. He stared, stone-faced, at Little Al.

"That answers my question," Little Al said.

Rudy moaned. "I bet she found out about Maury," he said. "I bet she's in there telling Dad all about it right now."

Little Al gave him a poke in the ribs. "How would she know? You think Maury Worthington's gonna march up to her and tell her he fell for a stunt like that?"

"That just shows what you two know."

Rudy looked up at Hildy Helen, who was easing herself down the stairs by clinging to the banister and hopping on one foot.

"What are you doing out of bed?" he said.

"I'm sick of being stuck up there and missing out on everything," she said. "Besides, you two need me to set you straight."

"About what?" Rudy said.

"Miss Tibbs and Dad are in there keeping company. Anybody with eyes can see that."

"Keeping company?" Rudy said.

Little Al sniffed. "You mean, like spoonin'?"

"What does that mean?" Rudy asked. "Would somebody speak English?"

Hildy Helen sighed the way she always did when she had to explain the obvious to her brothers. "They've got eyes for each other. Do you really think they're in there talking about us all the time? I don't."

Rudy stared at her. "You mean . . . like Miss Tibbs is Dad's . . . girl?"

"Says you!" Little Al said.

"Shhh! Both of you!" Hildy Helen hissed.

"You're makin' that up, Hildy Hutchinson," Rudy said. "I hope you are, anyway. That's the most disgusting thing I can think of."

"I don't know," Little Al said, head cocked to one side. "That Miss Dollface, she's a looker."

"But her and Dad?" Rudy said. His voice squeaked upward. "That would be awful. She's our teacher!"

"Oh, yeah," Little Al said.

"Yeah," Hildy Helen said. "I think we've got bigger problems than Rudy getting caught at tricking Maury Worthington."

"And how!" Rudy said. He was about to add that maybe they ought to start a campaign to fill Miss Tibbs's head full of all of their father's worst qualities when the library door opened. All three children flattened themselves against the banister, ears standing practically on end.

"They're muttering," Hildy Helen said in disgust. "I can't hear a thing they're saying."

"See if they kiss," Little Al said as he leaned out to watch them disappear toward the front door.

"Lay off!" Rudy said, pulling him back. "If they do, I don't want to know!"

"Me neither," Hildy Helen said. Then she shuddered as if a snake had just crawled across her lap.

They were all still sitting in stunned silence when the front door closed and a voice called out, "Rudy! Get down here—now! On the double! Let's go!"

"Oops," Hildy Helen said. Her eyes rounded at Rudy. "You want us to come with you?"

Rudy shook his head. "No use everybody getting yelled at. Just wait for me up in our room."

"Gotcha," Little Al said. "Buck up, Rudolpho. You can take it."

"Tell him you did it for me," Hildy Helen said. "I should take part of the punishment for—"

"Rudolph! Immediately!"

"Go," Little Al whispered. "He starts callin' you Rudolph, you know you're in for it."

Rudy tried to collect himself as he went slowly down the steps to the library. It was pretty clear by the look on his father's face that he didn't have romance on his mind. His small, dark eyes were glittering behind his glasses, and he'd raked his hand through his wavy, gray-streaked hair so many times it was standing on end in the front. When Rudy appeared, Dad nodded toward the library and waved him in. By the time they were sitting face-to-face at the long study table, Dad had loosened his wide necktie and rolled up the sleeves of his striped shirt. This was Jim Hutch-inson's way of getting down to business. It made Rudy's stomach churn.

But Dad's eyes were sad somehow as he leaned back in the leather chair and studied Rudy's face. "I thought you'd changed, son," he said. "I thought your class clown days were over."

"They are," Rudy said. He swallowed hard, and he wasn't act-ing this time. "I don't joke around in the classroom anymore."

"Don't turn this into a game of cat and mouse, Rudy," Dad said. His voice was suddenly weary. "Miss Tibbs told me what hap-pened to Maury Worthington. Why would you pull a stunt like that after all the things you've learned?"

Rudy didn't bother to ask how Miss Tibbs had found out, or what made everybody so sure he had done it. So far Dad wasn't threatening bodily punishment, and Rudy wanted to keep it that way.

"He tripped Hildy Helen during her dance, and that's how she got hurt," Rudy said. "I had to do something."

"Did you now?" said Dad. "You being detective, judge, jury, and jail keeper all in one?"

"We all knew he did it!" Rudy burst out. "But nobody's gonna be able to prove it, which means he won't get punished—so I had to do something!"

"You couldn't just accuse him to his face? You had to put him in physical danger?"

"I just convinced him to stick his tongue on the metal. It wasn't like I wanted him to step out in front of a train—"

"Have you ever had your tongue stuck to a piece of frozen metal?" Dad said.

Rudy couldn't help but grin. "No. I'm not that stupid."

Dad's eyebrows shot up, and Rudy immediately shook his head. If he didn't back off on this one, he'd find himself outside with his own tongue permanently affixed to the Pierce Arrow. Dad was big on the punishment fitting the crime.

"Are you the least bit sorry, Rudy?" his father said. "Just tell me that."

Rudy started to automatically shake his head again, but he couldn't. Instead, he studied the shiny tabletop carefully. "I guess I should be," he said finally. "But I'm not. I don't feel guilty at all. I mean—don't you get what you deserve when you're not a Christian?"

"I don't follow you," Dad said.

"At the table tonight, you were talking about how everything in Europe is such a mess and people here are afraid of people from Europe taking us over."

"I don't get the connection."

"Well, I was thinking, if they were all Christians like us Americans, they wouldn't be having all those problems. Just like Maury. He gets what he deserves because he obviously doesn't use Jesus as his model."

"Like you do," Dad said.

"Sure."

"Where in the Bible does it say Jesus ever tricked anybody into sticking their tongue to a—"

"It doesn't say we should vacuum the rugs every day with an electric sweeper either," Rudy said. He pointed to the many electrical plug outlets with their little brass covers that lined the baseboard in the library. "But we do it."

Dad ran his hands through his hair yet again and looked at Rudy with tired eyes. "Tomorrow after school," he said.

Rudy held his breath. Here it came. The punishment. *Why didn't I just say I was sorry?* he thought. *Now it's gonna be worse—*

"I want you to come to my office," Dad went on. "You're going to go with me to meet a new client."

Rudy waited. Dad pushed his chair back and stood up.

"Good night, now," he said. "Go straight to bed."

"That's it?" Rudy wanted to say. But this time he held his tongue and escaped to his room. He collapsed in relief on the bed between Hildy Helen and Little Al, the good news spilling out.

"That Mr. Hutchie, he's a prince," Little Al said. "If my stepfather had punished me like that, I'd still be livin' in Little Italy."

"Don't get too excited," Hildy Helen said.

Rudy propped up on his elbow. "Why not?"

"Because sometimes Dad's non-punishments are worse than getting your hide tanned."

Rudy's heart began to sink. "That's right," he said.

"Nah, I think that's all there is to it," Little Al said. "Maybe he figures you're right and he wants to let you off easy."

"Don't count on it," Hildy Helen said.

Rudy didn't. It was a good thing, too, because the next day proved she was right.

✝ ◦✝◦ ✝

Chapter Four

*T*he bad day started off when Rudy got to the breakfast table. Aunt Gussie looked up at him over her raisin toast and said, "Your father left a message for you, Rudolph. Something he forgot to tell you last night."

Rudy could feel Little Al and Hildy Helen holding their breath on either side of him.

"You are to apologize to Maurice Worthington before the day is over," Aunt Gussie said. "And you are to make certain that Miss Tibbs hears you."

"Would somebody pass the butter?" Hildy Helen said out loud. But her eyes were saying, "Told you so."

"I wish Dad had just gone ahead and tanned my hide," Rudy moaned as the three made their way through the icy slush to school. Hildy limped along, pretending her ankle didn't hurt at all.

"I'd take a beatin' anytime to sayin' anything to Maury Worthington except 'Go suck an egg!' " Little Al said.

"Don't say I didn't warn you," Hildy Helen said.

"Oh, hush up," Rudy said.

"Now, this is a sad-lookin' crew, it is!"

They all looked up to see Officer O'Dell smiling down out of

33

his weather-creased face. A lifetime of winters with freezing days like this had made those lines down his cheeks, but Rudy thought the lines kept him from looking stiff and mean the way most policemen did.

"Nobody died, God forbid?" the officer said.

"I wish I would," Rudy muttered.

At once Officer O'Dell's face darkened, and Rudy groaned inside. *Can't I say anything right anymore?* he thought.

"Never say that, lad," said the policeman, "even in jest. This city is a bad enough place without your fillin' your head with such thoughts. That's just why I stopped you this mornin', as a matter of fact."

"Did somebody die?" Hildy Helen said. She stood uncomfortably on one foot and looked as if she were trying not to wince.

"Not anybody you know—and I'd like to keep it that way." He motioned for them to come closer, and they did. He was so tall that their shoulders barely reached the belt he always wore with his billy club swinging from it.

"All right now," he said, "I want you three to be extra careful when you're out on the streets like this. There's been word at the station that the gangs—Capone's and Moran's—are gettin' more and more violent by the day. They're not just gunnin' down each other now. They're shootin' from their automobiles and hittin' innocent bystanders. Who's to say one of them couldn't be you?"

"Then there's only one thing to do," Rudy said. "We're gonna have to stay home from school." He grinned and started to turn on his heel, but Officer O'Dell took him by the shoulder. The policeman's leathery face was stern.

"This is no laughin' matter, lad," he said. "There's a whole race of gangsters runnin' amok. They have ice cubes for hearts and the appetites of cannibals. Nobody's safe in their jungle, not even you."

Rudy felt his face burning, even in the frosty air.

"Their gunmen hide in the shadows. Those trains roarin' over our heads can drown out your screams. It's worse than a jungle, I tell you. It's all about greed and revenge, it is, and it's only a matter of time until it'll lead to a massacre, you mark my words."

Rudy had never seen merry Officer O'Dell get quite that worked up, even the time the officer had been shot saving Rudy's life. Rudy found his own heart pounding fearfully inside his chest. He hated to be scared.

"I'm not worried," Rudy said. He pointed to the badge on the left side of the officer's coat. "We have you to protect us. You've done it before!"

But Officer O'Dell didn't smile. "The police are powerless to intervene in the gang wars, lad," he said. "That's the shame of it."

There wasn't time to ask why. In the distance, the first warning bell rang, and the three children edged anxiously toward it.

"You just be careful, all of you," Officer O'Dell said as he waved them away. "I know how you like to roam. Stay out of bad neighborhoods, d'y'hear?"

The kids nodded as they backed away and then turned to hurry the rest of the way to Felthensal, with Hildy hobbling more than ever. Rudy was sure he heard Officer O'Dell mutter behind them, "The neighborhood you live in is bad enough, and why a rich woman like Gustavia Nitz doesn't move to a safer location I'll never know."

Rudy looked around anxiously as he hustled after Hildy Helen and Little Al. Prairie Avenue had at one time been the most luxurious place to live in all of Chicago—lined with mansions built by people like Field, the department store founder; Armour, the meat-packing tycoon; and Pullman, creator of the Pullman railroad cars. Each home had been filled with fine furniture and great works of art. But since about 1900, Aunt Gussie had told them, everyone had begun moving to the North Side, leaving Prairie Avenue under a cloud of dilapidation and neglect. Now, in 1928,

Aunt Gussie's was one of the few houses left, and the only one that still looked like its former self—proud and magnificent spread over three lots on the corner of Prairie and 18th Street.

Sure, the sidewalk in front of it was cracked and broken, and the yards down the street were filled with broken fireplaces and choked with weeds. But it was the only home where Rudy had ever been truly happy. He wasn't ready to think about leaving it—not when he'd just gotten settled. In fact, that bothered him more than the idea of being shot at by a passing car full of mobsters.

Although he already had enough to worry about, not the least of which was staying vertical while skidding across the ice to get to class on time, he was nervous enough to bring it up with Hildy Helen as they were hanging their coats up in the cloakroom.

"You don't think Aunt Gussie would ever move away from Prairie Avenue, do you?" he said.

She stopped examining her ankle and looked up at him. "Don't be a goof, Rudy. Of course not. Everybody else gave up and ran away, but she never will. I've heard her say it."

That was good enough for the moment. Now he could turn to the other things he had to wrestle with. The first was how he was going to apologize to Maury Worthington without dying of humiliation—or throwing up. The very thought made the raisin toast gurgle in his stomach.

Naturally, it was impossible to concentrate on learning how to outline with Roman numerals, and when Little Al whispered across the aisle, "You gotta help me, Rudolpho! This stuff looks like Greek to me," Rudy was more lost than Al was.

And doing a multiplication problem on the chalkboard was out of the question, even with three tries. Miss Tibbs quietly sent Rudy back to his seat and went on to the next person. He could hear Maury and "the boys" snickering in the back of the room.

When the bell finally rang for first recess, Miss Tibbs came to his desk and gently pushed Rudy back into it.

"Wait here for a few minutes, Rudy," she said.

Little Al loitered, but Miss Tibbs shooed him out and Hildy Helen and the rest of their friends with them. The only other person she detained was Maury. Rudy prayed as hard as he could. *Please, God, let her make me apologize now, with nobody else around. Please let this be over.* He immediately felt better. God had pretty much proven that He was on Rudy's side and not on Maury's. That, Rudy figured, was what happened when you were really a Christian.

"I think we'd better get this over with, Rudy," Miss Tibbs said, "or you're never going to learn your Roman numerals—or anything else, for that matter."

"Get what over with?" Maury said. His big lower lip sagged nearly to his chest, which was heaving angrily. "I didn't do nothin'. It was all him!"

"Calm yourself, Maury," Miss Tibbs said. "This is part of Rudy's consequences. You had yours when you stuck your tongue on that frosted metal."

"Consequences for what?" Maury said. His face didn't know whether to be confused or angry, so it twitched comically back and forth. For once, though, Rudy wasn't amused.

"For baiting people," Miss Tibbs said, "but that isn't the point. Rudy did something he shouldn't have, and he's ready to apologize to you. Rudy, would now be a good time for that?"

It would have been an excellent time. In fact, there could have been no better way to set this up, and Rudy wanted to hug Miss Tibbs—well, almost. But with one look at the big bully's face, Rudy felt all traces of remorse disappear. Maury was sneering so hard, his upper lip was practically stuffed up his nose, and there was pure glee in his eyes. Rudy went from wanting to hug Miss Tibbs to wanting to slug Maury Worthington, all in one turn of the head. He felt his own upper lip curling.

"Rudy?" Miss Tibbs said. "Now is the time."

Rudy opened his mouth, but nothing would come out. All he could see was Maury sticking his big foot out and tripping Hildy Helen, making it so she could barely walk, much less dance. Then he saw himself cowering here like a whipped dog while Maury laughed at him and got away with everything.

Rudy shook his head.

"What is it?" Miss Tibbs said.

"I can't do it," Rudy said.

"Why not?"

"Because."

"Ru-dy . . . " Miss Tibbs was using her warning voice, and Maury was all but tapping his clumsy foot, but Rudy couldn't get anything out.

"He has to say he's sorry!" Maury said.

"If you want me to say I'm sorry, then all right!" Rudy dropped dramatically to one knee and clasped his hands in front of his chest. "Maurice, I must have an ice cube for a heart and the appetite of a cannibal to ever have done such a thing to you! Please, Maurice, I beg your forgiveness, even though I'm unworthy of it."

He bowed his head to keep Miss Tibbs from seeing him gnash his teeth. Above him there was a stunned silence. He half expected Maury to sock him one, right there in front of Miss Tibbs. But suddenly there was a grunt, and Rudy looked up. Maury was looking down at him and nodding.

"That's more like it," he said. "Now don't you forget it."

"Maury, that will be enough," Miss Tibbs said. "Go on out to recess now."

Maury grunted again and gave Rudy one more long, look-who's-boss-again glare before he ambled out of the room with his arms held out to his sides like a championship boxer.

"Rudy," Miss Tibbs said when Maury was gone.

Rudy tried to get his eyes to look innocent. Hildy Helen could do it so well, but he'd never been good at it. Miss Tibbs certainly wasn't buying it.

"You didn't mean a word of that, did you?" she said.

Rudy shook his head.

"Why not? I thought better of you."

"Because I'm not sorry," Rudy said. "He's doesn't act like a Christian, and he deserved it."

She opened her mouth as if to say something else, but she snapped it closed. "Go on out to recess," she said stiffly. "And from now on, let *me* dole out what people deserve, all right?"

It suddenly felt as cold in the room as it was outside, and Rudy was glad to hurry out into the hallway, where he ran head-on into Maury.

"I heard what you said in there," he said to Rudy between clenched teeth.

Rudy forced himself not to swallow. He looked nonchalantly at Maury. "So?" he said.

"So it ain't over. Just you remember, it ain't over." He stomped off down the hall.

"Thanks for makin' me better than him," Rudy said softly to God.

As Rudy waited for the downtown bus that afternoon to go to his father's office on Dearborn Street, he made up his mind to feel better. After all, the apology was over. And despite her pain, Hildy Helen had gotten through her dance at rehearsal without missing a step, which had made Dorothea's pale face go blotchy with the anger she was holding back.

Now there was only Dad's "punishment" to endure, and how bad could that be—going to see a new client? After all, Little Al had been one of Dad's clients, and besides, knowing how wrapped up his father usually got in his cases, he had probably forgotten he'd intended to discipline Rudy this afternoon. In fact, Rudy half expected Jim Hutchinson would look up from his desk and say,

"What are you doing here, Rudy?"

Yeah, everything's all right, he told himself. *I gotta remember, I'm a Christian. God's on my side.* He wriggled into a bus seat and busied himself looking out the window for faces to draw when he got home later.

As they traveled west on 16th Street, Rudy noticed that the people braving the cold fell into two groups. One group seemed annoyed by the cold, hunching up their shoulders and glaring at the frosty air as if winter were a personal affront. The other group refused to acknowledge its presence at all as they held their heads high and let the frigid afternoon nip unnoticed at their noses. As the bus drew nearer to the Loop—the center of downtown—all of them were jostling each other rudely as they hurried along.

Rudy could never understand why people made such a big deal out of the temperature. When it was cold, you put on your overcoat and muffler and mittens and you went about your business—especially down here in the city, where there were so many interesting things to see. He set himself to wondering which part of town his father would take him to.

Jim Hutchinson was a pro bono lawyer, which meant he took clients who couldn't afford to pay him. Aunt Gussie took care of that. It made for interesting work for Dad, and by the time the bus driver called out over his shoulder, "Dearborn Street," Rudy was almost excited about what lay ahead.

The bus stopped a block from the Franklin Printing Building, where Dad's office was located, and Rudy headed toward it. Although it was only 3:30, the sky was already darkening, and streetlights were winking on, making fuzzy circles of yellow on the ice below. Rudy took in as much of the scene as he could. Throngs of office workers and shoppers were hurrying on their way to streetcar stops or commuter train stations. In the bumper-to-bumper autos, drivers were blowing their horns. The El trains clattered and roared as they sped by on their elevated tracks. Rudy could smell the billowing puffs of smoke pouring out of factory smokestacks beyond. Shop signs were beckoning passersby with their bright words, such as "Suits for Men $21" and "Kotz's Shoes—Exercise Your Credit With Easy Payment Plans" and "Weiss's Restaurant for Good Food."

Once at the Franklin Building, Rudy pushed his way through the revolving door. His father had pointed out to him more than once that all the workers passed through this front door, no matter what their station, because that was the American way. All men might be created equal, but Rudy was feeling decidedly superior as he stood in front of the elevator and watched the floor indicator arrow above the doors, between the two plaster cherubs.

I might be here to get punished for what I did to Maury, he thought, *but even Miss Tibbs knew he had it coming. She as much as told him so.*

He brushed aside the memory of the chilly way she had sent him out to the playground, and he stepped into the elevator.

Bridget was at the typewriter when Rudy got to the office. She worked for Dad several afternoons a week, and she was evidently hard at work today. She barely nodded her curly red head at Rudy before she stuck a pencil in her mouth, wheeled her chair over to a filing cabinet, and started digging through it.

"Bet you wonder what I'm doing here, huh?" Rudy said, eyeing the bowl of gumdrops on the corner of her desk.

"Nope," she said around the pencil. "Your dad's in there waiting for you. I'd hurry it up if I were you."

So much for Dad not remembering, Rudy thought. But he was undaunted as he scooped two gumdrops into his mouth and tapped on Dad's door.

"Don't take your coat off, Rudy," Dad said. He already had his topcoat on and was reaching for the fedora hanging on the hat rack. "It's going to take some time to get out there because of rush hour." He glanced at his black-banded wristwatch and tucked a fountain pen into his pocket.

"Where are we going?" Rudy said.

"Chicago Jerusalem," Dad said.

"Huh?"

"Lawndale."

"Never heard of it."

Dad squinted a little behind his glasses, but he took hold of Rudy's shoulder and steered him toward the door. "You're going to know a lot about it after today," he said.

Rudy wasn't sure he liked the sound of that. But he waited until he and Dad had boarded their train before he asked any questions. Aunt Gussie had said a hundred times that Chicago's mass transit system always had fewer seats than it did passengers, so finding a place to park oneself while the train sped across Chicago took most of his attention. Once he was clinging safely to an overhead strap, he said, "How come they call this place we're going to 'Chicago Jerusalem'?"

"Because about half the Jewish population of Chicago lives there," Dad said.

Rudy pushed his glasses up his nose. "Your client's Jewish?" he said.

"He is."

"Why are you defending a Jewish person?"

Dad squinted his eyes at Rudy again, scrunching them tighter this time. "You don't think I should represent a Jew?" he said.

"Well, he's not a Christian."

"Hmm," Dad said. "You know something, Rudy, this is a better idea than I thought. You're going to learn a lot today."

Rudy didn't like the sound of that either, so he quickly changed the subject. "Hey, Dad," he whispered. "How come everyone has their faces buried in the newspaper?"

Dad looked around the train car, where every head was hidden behind an early edition of the *Chicago Tribune* or the *Chicago Daily News*.

Dad grunted. "They're trying to catch the 1:30 quotations from Wall Street."

"Huh?"

"Everybody's wrapped up in the stock market, son."

"Oh, that."

"Yes, that. Look at them, Rudy."

Rudy did, but he didn't see anything particularly strange about any of them.

"They've all spent the money they've saved, and then they've borrowed money, and they've borrowed on their borrowings, all to get a few little pieces of paper that make them partners in American industry."

"Huh?" Rudy said.

His father smiled faintly and patted his shoulder. "Someday I'll explain it all to you, son. I hope I won't be explaining an economic disaster."

"You think there's gonna be a disaster?" Rudy said.

"I think that's what it's going to take to shake the public out of the stock market, but that opinion doesn't make me very popular."

As if to prove it, the man beside Rudy peered at Jim Hutchinson over his *Chicago Tribune* and scowled. Rudy was glad when his father finally said, "This is our stop."

They stepped off the train into a quiet neighborhood with a wide street, lined on either side by brick homes and apartments with lights shining onto the darkening street.

At least they have electricity here, Rudy thought. He knew Chicago's West Side was made up of neighborhoods where people from the same foreign countries lived together. Little Al had come from Little Italy, and at Hull House he had met people from Greektown and Chinatown and the Mexican part of the city, so he was used to things being "un-American."

But un-Christian, that was something he wasn't accustomed to. He felt more out of place here than he ever had on the streets of Little Italy.

The yellow street sign on the corner announced that this was Douglas Boulevard. Aside from that, he couldn't read another thing he saw in print. It all seemed to be written in a bunch of squiggles and curlicues that made no sense at all. Only by looking in the windows could he tell what the shops were—bookstores, restaurants, delis, and fish stores. He was so busy staring at a sign on a flower shop, he nearly ran smack into a bearded man in a big, fuzzy hat with its sides up. It made him look as if he were about to take flight.

"Sorry," Rudy said.

"Yah," said the man, and then he added something else in a sing-songy voice that made Rudy turn and stare at him until he disappeared into a dark door.

"What's that place he's going into?" Rudy whispered to his father.

"A Yiddish theater," Dad said.

"What's Yiddish?" Rudy said. He hoped it wasn't something to eat. It sounded disgusting. "And what's that place?" He pointed to a large, elaborate-looking building with more of the funny writing scrawled on its sign.

"That's a synagogue."

"Sin-a-what? Is that where you go when you sin?"

Dad smiled. "Something like that," he said. "There are about 40 orthodox synagogues here."

"Why so many?"

"Because a Jew isn't allowed to ride in a vehicle on the Sabbath. He has to walk to the temple."

Dad hurried on. Rudy quickened his steps to follow his father. There were more people on the sidewalk here, and most of them were men with scraggly beards down to their chests, who stared openly at the Hutchinsons.

"Don't these people believe in razors?" Rudy whispered to Dad.

Dad just nodded vaguely and pointed to more unintelligible writing painted on the window of what was apparently a grocery store, though Rudy couldn't identify any of the meats that hung there.

"Here we are," Dad said, and he turned abruptly into the doorway.

Once inside, Rudy glanced around at the crates of fresh vegetables, the bins of fruit, and the jars with strange clumps floating in them. He wrinkled his nose. "It smells funny in here," he said.

"Keep your voice down," Dad said. His voice had a rare sharpness. "Mr. Levitsky owns this store. Show some respect now."

Rudy tugged at the back of his father's overcoat. "Why do we have to respect these people?" he said. "Aren't they the ones who killed Jesus?"

Dad didn't answer but instead turned to someone who was peering at them from over the top of the counter, staring just the way everyone else had.

Rudy surveyed the contents of the store. Sausages the size of vacuum cleaner hoses hung from the ceiling, and the counter was lined with jars containing fat pickles floating in brine. Even the boxes on the shelves were covered with that odd writing. If Rudy's nerves hadn't been chewing at the inside of his stomach, he would have studied the script a little more carefully, just to see if he could copy it in his sketchbook.

"Hello there," Dad said to the person behind the counter.

You really think he's going to understand you? Rudy thought. *I bet he doesn't speak English.*

But the person said, "May I help you?" in a polite voice, and Rudy turned quickly to look.

It was a chunky girl, not quite Rudy and Hildy Helen's age, and the minute Rudy looked at her, his artistic side took over. He had to draw a sketch of this girl.

She had a thick head of hair that curled at her temples. Hildy Helen would have squealed over it, wishing her straight mop would do the same. The girl had very bright, sharp eyes that regarded them with suspicion. But that wasn't what captured Rudy. It was her face; her features were ruddy and big and full, and they all seemed to stand out on her face. It would be a challenge to draw her, because he couldn't decide whether it would be funniest to exaggerate her nose or her lips or her cheeks.

If his father thought she was funny looking, he didn't let on. He just as politely said, "Is Mr. Levitsky in?"

The girl nodded solemnly.

"Could you please tell him he has someone here to see him?"

The girl continued to stare, but Rudy saw her suspicious eyes go fearful.

"I told him I would be here," Dad said.

At that, the girl leaped away from the counter and dove through a narrow curtain that seemed to lead into some back room. Rudy could hear excited gibberish being exchanged, and then the curtain was ruffled again.

A man emerged, whiskered down to the bib of his white apron but otherwise looking like a copy of the girl. It was as if she had run into the back room and come out with a false beard. Rudy could only stare. In his hand, the man held a pistol, and he pointed it straight at Jim Hutchinson.

✟ ✟ ✟

Chapter Five

*A*lmost with one motion, Dad shoved Rudy to the floor and raised his hands into the air.

"Mr. Levitsky!" he said. "It's James Hutchinson. I'm the attorney you sent for!"

Rudy waited for a shot to crack through the store, but there was only a startled gasp, and then a high-pitched cry. "Mr. Hutchinson! Can you imagine such a thing?"

The man's voice was thick with an accent Rudy didn't recognize. *It must be from talking that Yiddish stuff*, Rudy thought. He stood up warily to see Mr. Levitsky grasping his father's hands.

"I promised you I'd come this afternoon," Dad said. "I always try to keep my promises."

"Yah, yah. We thought you were one of those men. Come in—sit down. We'll eat."

Rudy's stomach rumbled sickly, but Dad smiled and nodded as if they'd been offered banana splits. Mr. Levitsky yelped something over his shoulder. Immediately a large woman with a straight line for a mouth appeared. There was more yelping of gibberish, and she disappeared. To his dismay, she was back within blinking time, carrying a tray that practically groaned with hunks of slimy-looking fish.

"You like pickled herring?" Mr. Levitsky said.

Before Rudy could say, "I'm not hungry," Dad said, "I haven't had pickled herring in years!" He winked slyly behind his glasses. "It's kosher, of course?"

"Such a question! Is it kosher? It's kosher, all right!"

Rudy watched, stomach turning, as the big woman, who must be Mrs. Levitsky, placed what looked like an entire fish on a plate and handed it to him. He promised himself he'd never turn his nose up at Quintonia's turnip greens again.

I'll just push it around with my fork and drop some of it in my napkin while they're talking, Rudy decided.

But not a word was spoken as Jim Hutchinson plunged his fork into the pickled herring and took his first bite. In fact, neither Mr. nor Mrs. Levitsky ate a thing. They just leaned in and watched Dad's face as if for telltale traces of dislike. Rudy stuffed a slimy hunk into his own mouth so he could get it down before they set their sights on him. It squished against his teeth. He quickly grabbed up the mug that Mrs. Levitsky had placed near him and washed the mouthful down as soon as he could.

It seemed to take forever for the Levitskys to be satisfied that Dad had eaten as much as he possibly could and had enjoyed each morsel more than the one before it. Only then did the conversation begin.

"So, tell me your story, Mr. Levitsky," Dad said. "How can I help you?" Rudy sighed and leaned back in his chair. This was bound to be boring, but anything was better than eating the foul fish while people watched.

"For this, I must start from the beginning," Mr. Levitsky said.

"Of course," Dad said.

Rudy groaned silently.

"My father came to this country when I was a baby. There was so much poverty in Poland that he thought to make a better life for us here, yah?"

"And was it better?" Dad said.

"Such a question! Was it better? he asks." He turned briefly to Rudy as if expecting some kind of response, and then just as quickly he jerked his thinly bearded chin away. "We were poor, yah. We lived on Maxwell Street—to the south of here, you know."

"I know it well," Dad said. "My aunt used to take me to shop there." He turned to Rudy. "You could buy anything on Maxwell Street—kosher meats, dry goods, matzo. And then there were the pushcarts and the stands, open dawn 'til dark." Dad sighed. "I can still smell the garlic, the cheeses, the onions."

Rudy stayed perfectly still for fear that the slightest move from him would send Mrs. Levitsky scurrying to the kitchen for a trayful.

"My father worked in the meat-packing plant," Mr. Levitsky said. "We lived in a boardinghouse. There were 13 of us in one room. Ach, the stench, you can't imagine it."

Please don't ask me to, Rudy thought.

"There was the stink of livestock manure, the sausage—the black smoke belching from the smokestacks. But my father, he kept his eyes on heaven and his head where it belonged, with his own people. Slowly, slowly, we flourished in Chicago."

Anything would be better than what they were doing, Rudy thought. The description of the smell was threatening to bring the pickled herring up for another round.

"We were the shtetl Jews," Mr. Levitsky went on. "We had suffered the pogroms in the old country."

"Can you tell Rudy about the pogroms?" Dad said.

"Such a question! Can I tell about the pogroms? I can tell about the pogroms, all right. But does he want to hear? That is the question."

Rudy was about to shake his head until it shook off his shoulders, but Dad gave him a warning squint from behind his glasses.

"Sure," Rudy said.

"Well, I won't tell you. You'll have nightmares. Nightmares is what you'll have."

Mr. Levitsky lapsed into a sudden silence and stared down at Dad's empty plate until his eyes grew wet. Rudy looked in panic at his father, but Dad just nodded and said quietly, "A *pogrom* was an organized massacre of Jews. Thousands were killed, just because they were Jewish."

"Oh," Rudy said.

"So, so, so," Mr. Levitsky said. He took a deep breath and mopped his eyes with a corner of his apron. "Nothing could be so bad here, yah, not after that. Soon we moved into a tenement with no light and not too many baths. But it was brick, and it kept out the cold. My mother took in lodgers—used the same bed for a baker by day and a butcher at night."

"The hot bed system!" Dad said. He looked as if he were enjoying every minute of this. Rudy wearily planted his elbows on the table.

"Finally there was enough money for Papa to start his own grocery." Mr. Levitsky gave a satisfied nod as if the rest were history.

"And you've carried on the family business," Dad said, looking around admiringly at the crowded shelves.

"Yah. When he died, we moved here. Most of the Jews were gone from Maxwell Street by then." He shook his head sadly. "I don't even go back there now. It's too sad—too sad."

Rudy thought he was going to start with the tears again, but Mr. Levitsky gave his head a stubborn shake and said, "So, so, so" at least 20 times. "It's a good life here in Lawndale," he said. "We are middle-class now." His eyes took on a proud sheen that quickly faded as if his next thought had pulled a veil over them. "And then this thing happens. There are problems here. There is crime. The goyim come in and throw stones and pull the old men's beards. But I never thought—can you imagine it? I never thought—"

He paused again, and Dad respectfully lowered his eyes until Mr. Levitsky could go on. Rudy tried not to squirm.

"I never thought shame would come to my family," Mr. Levitsky said finally.

"What shame, Mr. Levitsky?" Dad said.

"No, call me Uriah, please." He patted Dad's hand soundly. "You're a good boy, anybody can see that."

Dad nodded. Rudy looked from one of them to the other. It was as if they'd made friends right before his eyes and he hadn't seen it happening.

"The shame, ah, the shame," Mr. Levitsky said. "Such a question. I run an honest store here, Mr. Hutchinson."

"Jim."

"Jim, I run an honest store here. We make enough to live and to give money to the synagogue for the Jews still in our country, yah?"

Rudy watched the man's face. *I always heard Jews were stingy and dishonest*, he thought.

"And I would like to continue to do so in peace." The man pulled miserably at his beard. "But the other day—it was three days ago now—I sent Nathaniel out to buy horseradish from Chaim Yenkel, across the street on the sidewalk."

"And who is Nathaniel?" Dad said.

"Ah, Nathaniel is my son. Fifteen years old, he is. And he's a good boy."

"I'm sure he is."

Uriah pointed his sharp eyes at Dad for a moment, as if looking to make sure Jim Hutchinson was really convinced of Nathaniel's goodness.

"He wasn't gone a minute—ah, maybe two—who can tell," Mr. Levitsky went on, "and then I heard them."

"Who?" Dad said.

"*Who?* No, *what!* The shots, the shots."

"Gunshots?"

"Of course, gunshots! Such a question!" Uriah's face darkened above his beard, and he plucked at the whiskers fretfully. "There were shots and screams. I ran out like a madman, and it was all over."

This time Dad just waited for him to go on.

"There was the boy lying on the sidewalk with the blood running from him. An Italian boy, barely 14. And there was Nathaniel, standing over him. His face was white. He was shaking like a leaf. That's when I saw it. That's when I saw the gun lying on the ground at his feet."

He dropped it there? Rudy wondered. By this time, he'd laid his forearms on the table and was leaning toward Mr. Levitsky.

"It was nothing but confusion. The whole street was *meshugena,*" Uriah said. "That is craziness," he said to Rudy with a nod. He closed his eyes as he talked. "Nathaniel couldn't speak a word. Always he talks—the ideas, the questions. But now, he just stood there like a dead man."

"Was the Italian boy dead?" Dad said.

Uriah shook his head. "The ambulance came, and then the police. I said to Nathaniel, 'Nathaniel, you must speak! You must tell them what happened here.'" Uriah closed his eyes again. "Always the talking with Nathaniel. But now he could barely speak a word."

"Did he tell them anything?" Dad said. His hand slipped inside his coat and he pulled out his fountain pen. His eyes were focused like a pair of headlights on Mr. Levitsky's face. There was none of the usual vagueness in his manner now.

"Ah, such a question! Did he tell them anything? He told them something, all right! He told them the boy who had been shot was one of the young Italians who had come up to him and spat at him because he didn't have his friends there to protect him."

Dad looked up sharply from making notes on the pad of paper he'd also extracted from his pocket. "What friends are those?"

"My Nathaniel, he's part of the Miller gang."

It was Rudy's turn to look up sharply. *It isn't bad enough the kid is Jewish?* he thought. *He's a mobster, too?*

"I'm not familiar with them," Dad said.

"They're good boys, all of them," Uriah said quickly. Once again he plucked at his beard. "They spend too much time at Davy Miller's pool hall on Roosevelt Road. I tell Nathaniel that. I tell him every day. But he says 'Pop'—Pop he calls me." He shook his head as if to rattle the right thoughts back into place. "He says, 'Pop, we have to stick together. We have to protect the neighborhood from the gentile gangs—the boys who come in from the outside and bother the yeshiva students.' "

"What's *yeshiva?*" Rudy wanted to ask, but he bit his tongue. In spite of himself, he was starting to become interested in the story. *I don't want to slow him down or we'll never hear what happened*, he thought. *It's probably not as good as it sounds, though. He's a Jew, after all.*

"Those gentile boys put gum in the beards of the old Jews," Uriah was saying. "They throw rocks. They push over the carts of poor men just trying to make a living. Can you imagine such a thing?"

Dad shook his head.

"Ah, so, so, so," Uriah said, "Nathaniel tells me, 'The Miller gang only strikes when we're attacked, Pop. We are only out to defend our neighborhood.' "

Suddenly this sounded so familiar, Rudy had to blink hard to make sure he was sitting in a grocery in Chicago Jerusalem and not in Little Italy listening to Little Al talk. Before Al had come to live at Aunt Gussie's, he'd told Rudy many times that he was only defending the Italian code of honor.

"The Italians were out looking for trouble that day," Uriah said. "That's what Nathaniel told the police."

"Did he shoot that Italian kid?"

Dad's pen scratched to a halt on his pad, and both men stared at Rudy. He didn't even know he'd blurted it out until the words had stung Mr. Levitsky right between the eyes.

"No!" Uriah said, pulling himself up in his chair until even his beard looked stiff. "Nathaniel said a car drove up just as he went out the door of the grocery—"

"What kind of car?" Dad said.

"A long, black car," Uriah said, searching the ceiling for the details. "And windows you can't see through, yah? As if someone had something to hide, yah? Always with the dark windows, those Italians—"

"And what about the car?" Dad said.

"It slowed down in front of the grocery," Uriah said. "Nathaniel told the police, you understand. And they asked so many questions, always with the questions. And Nathaniel said the car slowed down, and suddenly there was a gunshot, and the Italian boy was lying on the sidewalk groaning."

"Do you know the boy's name?" Dad said.

"Victor," Uriah said. His lip curled from beneath his beard "Victor Vedoli. I don't wish nobody harm, you understand."

"Of course not."

"But that boy—no, that boy's friends, the other Italians—they took off running." He shook his head. "The policemen left, and I thought it was done. I told Nathaniel, 'No more with the Miller gang!' But then, that same night, the police came back, this time with the other boys."

"The Italians?"

"Them. They stood here in this grocery—" Uriah pointed to a spot in front of the counter, where Mrs. Levitsky was now leaning and listening. Rudy noticed that the girl was peeking out from behind the curtain. When they all turned in her direction, she whipped the curtain closed.

"They stood there," Uriah said, still staring at the spot, "and they pointed their fingers at my Nathaniel and they told those policemen that he, my son, shot Victor Vedoli." Uriah's shoulders went limp. "And then they arrested him and took him off to jail."

Rudy had the urge to slump, too, though he didn't know why. *If Nathaniel shot somebody—maybe an old friend of Little Al's— why shouldn't he go to jail?* Rudy didn't see what his father could possibly do about this one.

"If it's not bad enough he's in the jail!" Uriah said, face going still darker as he turned back to them. "Since then, there have been threats to me and the rest of my family."

"Threats from whom?" Dad said.

"Men in silk suits, yah, driving up in their long cars with the lumps of their guns under their suits."

"How do they threaten you?" Dad said.

"They say I must pay them protection money to make sure no one damages my store. Then they tell me if I will agree to sell their liquor in this store—if I agree and can influence other shop- keepers to agree, perhaps these men can help my son."

Dad's pen paused. "And you have told them—?"

"Such a question! I cannot do that! I run an honest business here!" His dark face suddenly paled, and once again he slumped in his chair. "But if I do not, what will happen to my Nathaniel? That is the question. That is the question I ask you, Jim!"

Rudy looked head-on at his father. Surely he wasn't going to take on this case. It was all he could do not to grab his father's arm and drag him out of there. But he knew Dad. Anyone who had nowhere else to turn could count on Jim Hutchinson for help—even a Jew who'd shot someone.

But to his surprise, Dad didn't immediately jump up and shake Uriah's hand. Instead, he toyed for a moment with his pen, and then said, "Why did you come to me, Mr. Levitsky? I know you must have the means to hire someone. And why not one of your Jewish lawyers? They're highly respected as attorneys."

Uriah didn't even blink. "I had thought to do that. They come no better than Feodor Mishkin."

"That's true."

"But he told me himself I would be better off hiring a gentile. He says Nathaniel's case will not turn into politics that way."

"That's why Mishkin has the reputation he does," Dad said. "He's right. We don't want this to become Christian versus Jew."

"Yah," said Uriah. "Because we all know who will win, yah?"

Dad didn't answer. He went back to scribbling notes on his pad with his fountain pen. Rudy clutched the seat of his chair.

"Do you think those men in the car shot Victor Vedoli?" Dad said. "I'd like to consider any theories you might have."

"Such a question! Do I think? I think, all right!" Uriah's sharp black eyes narrowed to pencil points. "It was the mob, that is what I think. Maybe Al Capone or Moran."

Rudy was surprised that this old-world-looking man living in some part of the city Rudy had never heard of would know about Al Capone and Bugs Moran.

"I think, always the thinking—"

"Of course," Dad said. "But why would they shoot one of their own?"

"Accidents happen, yah? And now they blame it on a Jewish boy, who represents what they hate. Very convenient, yah?"

Dad didn't answer but scratched his pen across the paper once more and then abruptly put it away, stuffed the pad into his pocket, and put out his hand to Mr. Levitsky. "You can count on me, Uriah," he said.

Once more the Jew's eyes reddened and filled, and he clasped Dad's hand with both of his. "I knew you were a good boy," he said. "How can I thank you? Such a question! I cannot thank you. I can only say 'God bless you.' "

God? Rudy thought. *What is he talking about? The only way to God is Jesus, right? Questions. Always with the questions—* Rudy shook his head. He had to get out of here before he started talking like this man.

Dad stood up, still clasping hands with a grateful Uriah Levitsky, and assured him that he would be back as soon as he could gather more information. When he turned to bid Mrs. Levitsky good-bye, Rudy saw the curtain creep open again. So, evidently, did Mr. Levitsky.

"Isabel!" he yelped.

The curtain whipped shut over the funny little face.

"I never saw such a funny-looking girl," Rudy told Little Al and Hildy Helen later that night as they sat in the library doing their long division homework.

"Show us, Rudy," Hildy Helen said. She ripped a blank page from her notebook and slid it toward him. "Draw her."

Rudy sketched out Isabel Levitsky's protruding nose and full lips and serious stare, exaggerating each feature until both Little Al and Hildy Helen were howling.

"So she's a Jew, huh?" Little Al said.

Hildy Helen's brown eyes widened. "They're Jews?" she said. "I've never known anybody Jewish."

"And I don't want to know anybody Jewish," Rudy said. He felt himself squirming on the leather chair. "I wish Dad would just let those people solve their own problems."

"How come?" Little Al said.

But Rudy didn't have a chance to answer.

"Rudy," said a voice from the doorway. "I'd like to speak to you."

"Mad Dad! Mad Dad!" Picasso squawked from his cage.

"Uh-oh again," Hildy Helen whispered.

Rudy trailed out of the library after his father.

✝ ✦ ✝

Chapter Six

*T*he only light in the hallway came from the electric Christmas lights that Sol had strung. But as Rudy stood facing his father, there was enough light for him to see Dad's face. It wasn't happy.

"Rudy, you entirely missed the point of my taking you to Lawndale," he said.

"No, I didn't, Dad," Rudy said. "It was a punishment, believe me. Do you know how close I came to upchucking when I ate that—"

"It wasn't meant to be a punishment." Dad's voice was sharp. "It was intended to be an education."

"Then I learned, honest I did," Rudy said. He attempted a grin. "I know Yiddish isn't food and that pickled herring is—"

"*Enough.*"

It was the closest Rudy had ever heard his father come to yelling. Rudy sucked back his next funny reply and held his breath.

"Not only am I going to take this case, Rudy," Dad said through tightened teeth, "but you are going to help me with it."

"Me?"

"And Hildy Helen and Little Al as well."

"They'll hate me if you do that!"

Dad shook his head. "No, son, everyone will hate you if you don't get rid of those narrow, foolish views of yours." He put his fingers to the bridge of his nose and squeezed as he closed his eyes. "I can't for the life of me figure out where they came from. Although I shouldn't be surprised, leaving you and your sister to your own devices all your lives the way I did—"

"But since we came here, we've straightened up!" Rudy said. "I hardly ever wipe my nose on my sleeve or even dip girls' hair in inkwells anymore!"

"I'm talking about something much more serious than the neglect of your manners," Dad said.

"I'm a Christian now! I draw Jesus all the time. You haven't seen my sketchbook."

"You're a Christian," Dad said.

"Yeah!"

"Then let's make sure you behave like one. You're on this case with me, Rudy."

There was still anger in his father's eyes, and Rudy could feel some rage of his own bubbling up. "Can't it wait until after Christmas at least?" he said. "We've got the pageant coming up and all the other Christmas stuff. There's so many swell things to do, and suddenly I gotta help some Jewish kid? We don't even know if he's innocent!"

Dad's eyebrows shot up above the steel rims of his glasses. "Don't we?" he said. "I've checked into it. Where did Nathaniel get an expensive gun like that? And why would he drop the gun and stand there with it lying at his feet if he'd just shot someone? Wouldn't he have run away if he were guilty?"

"I don't know," Rudy said stubbornly. His stomach was churning, and it wasn't from the pickled herring this time. "We weren't there, so we don't even know what *really* happened."

"How often am I at the scene of the crime one of my clients supposedly committed?" Dad said. "I have to trust Uriah."

"But why?" Rudy said. "Aren't Jews supposed to be dishonest?"

Dad's face turned a deep shade of red, and for a moment, Rudy thought he was going to explode. But even as they stood there staring at each other, the color faded and Dad said quietly, "You have so much more to learn than I thought, Rudy. I need to start teaching you right away." He went briskly to the library door and pulled it open. Little Al and Hildy Helen lurched forward into the hall. Dad didn't look at all surprised.

"Tomorrow afternoon, right after school," Dad said, "all three of you are to meet me at my office. We're going back to Lawndale."

Little Al's and Hildy Helen's eyes narrowed at Rudy at the same time. "But, Dad!" Rudy said. "Just today, Officer O'Dell told us to stay out of bad neighborhoods."

"Come here, all of you," Dad said.

He charged into the library, with his chin jutting out.

"Mad Dad, mad Dad," Picasso muttered nervously.

Dad flung open the curtain on the front window and pointed out at the street, which was desolate except for the lone lamp at the corner.

"Look at Prairie Avenue," he said.

The three children gathered reluctantly at the window.

"It seems to me," Dad said, "that the Jews you're so busy looking down on have done a better job of keeping up their neighborhood than we have. If you aren't afraid to walk your street, you don't need to be afraid to walk theirs."

Rudy scowled out at the night. He'd used up all his chances. That was the end of it. They were going back to the Levitsky's tomorrow, and it was a lousy deal.

And then it got lousier. The next morning, Friday, Rudy and Little Al woke to Hildy Helen's wailing from her room down the hall.

"I *have* to go to school, Aunt Gussie!" she was crying. "The pageant is tonight, and I have to practice!"

"Not with that ankle, you don't. Look at it, Hildegarde. It's swollen to twice its size, and it's black-and-blue. You dance on that, and you won't be able to walk."

But she can't walk around in Lawndale on that ankle, either, can she? Rudy thought. Then he felt guilty.

He felt worse when, moments later, he saw the ankle itself. Aunt Gussie had it propped up on two pillows, and it looked like a big piece of that vacuum-cleaner-hose sausage, only blue. Quintonia blew in with a bowlful of something that smelled lemony.

"What's that stuff?" Hildy Helen said, wrinkling her nose.

"That 'stuff' is witch hazel, and it is the only way I'm going to allow you to go to school and try to dance," Aunt Gussie said. "Cooperate with Quintonia. Let her put that on, and then you stay off that ankle completely until you have to dance, do you hear me?"

Hildy Helen nodded eagerly.

"All right." Aunt Gussie stood up and went for the door. "I'm going to tell Sol to bring the car around. You are certainly not going to walk to school. And if it hurts even the least little bit while you are practicing, there will be no dancing tonight."

"I *have* to dance," Hildy Helen declared.

"We'll see," Aunt Gussie said firmly.

"Don't you worry," Quintonia said when she was gone. "You are gon' dance tonight, and you are gon' show that stuffy ol' Dorothea Worthington just what hoofin' is."

Little Al grinned and patted Quintonia on the back. "Have I told you I like a doll like you?" he said.

But Rudy wasn't so sure Quintonia was right. All day at school, Hildy Helen sat at her desk with her foot propped up on a box Miss Tibbs found for her, while Dorothea complained about the smell of the witch hazel. Hildy Helen didn't even go out for recess, and Rudy, Little Al, Earl, Fox, and Agnes Ann all stayed in with her. Hildy Helen smiled through it all and insisted that it didn't hurt a bit, but Rudy knew better. They weren't twins for nothing.

By that afternoon's rehearsal, Rudy's stomach was doing somersaults. He climbed to his spot on the risers and looked anxiously backstage where Hildy Helen was standing up for the first time that day and cautiously putting weight on her ankle. If it hurt, she wasn't showing it, because Dorothea was standing next to her, her hooked chin held up haughtily like some prima donna at the ballets Aunt Gussie had dragged them to.

But when the "snowflakes" started their twirls across the stage, Rudy could see the tears in his sister's eyes. It had to hurt, because the Hutchinson twins never cried in front of anybody.

Jesus? Rudy prayed. *You're gonna help her, aren't You? We are Christians, after all.* He was drawing a picture in his mind of Jesus standing on the top riser, waving His hand down in Hildy Helen's direction, when the music suddenly stopped and Miss Tibbs clapped her hands. Hildy Helen sat down immediately on the bottom riser.

"Maury," Miss Tibbs said, "what is so important that you and Al have to discuss it during the dance number?"

"Sorry, Miss Dollface," Little Al said. "It won't happen again."

"No, it won't," Miss Tibbs said briskly, "because if it does, I will take both of you out of the show all together. Is that understood?"

It was. In fact, the entire class nodded. Miss Tibbs hardly ever used a stern voice. When she did, there was no arguing.

She started the rehearsal again, and this time the snowflakes got through their entire dance. Rudy watched his sister as he hummed. She wasn't giving it everything she had, but even at that, she was 20 times—no, make that 40 times—better than

Dorothea. Dorothea knew it, too, because her nose and chin never stopped nearly touching each other as she grimaced behind Hildy. When the dance was over, Hildy Helen stole a glance up at Rudy. They exchanged smug smiles. Maybe this was going to work out after all.

Sol came to pick Hildy Helen up after school, but Little Al suggested that he and Rudy walk home. Although the snow was coming down in big cottony clumps, Rudy agreed. Little Al's eyes were shining with news.

"What's up?" Rudy said as they bowed their faces from the windy snowfall and made their way down Prairie.

"If Hildy Helen doesn't dance tonight—"

"She will!"

"Yeah—but what if her ankle's swole up more and Miss Gustavio won't let her? Did ya ever thinka that?"

"It isn't gonna happen," Rudy said.

"Yeah, well, where I grew up, you gotta have a just-in-case plan, if you know what I mean."

"So what's yours?" Rudy said.

"If Hildy Helen doesn't dance tonight, I'm gonna get Maury taken care of so he never thinks of messin' with us again."

"But what—"

"You wanna stay outta trouble?" Little Al said.

Rudy nodded.

"Then that's all you gotta know."

"Yeah, I guess you're right," Rudy said. He twisted his mouth. "I don't need Dad 'educating' me any more than he already is."

When they got home, Aunt Gussie and Quintonia examined Hildy Helen's ankle, did some more stuff to it, and deemed it to be in good enough shape for Hildy Helen to go to Lawndale with the boys and Dad if Sol drove them.

"Your father will hate that," Aunt Gussie said, "but it's either that or she doesn't go. I'm going to call him and tell him that."

As he climbed into the back of the Pierce Arrow, Rudy let the guilty thought pass through that this just might be their ticket out of Lawndale for today. Still, he couldn't help sulking as Sol wound the car through the traffic-swollen city streets. He'd rather be doing anything else but going back to that smelly grocery store and eating pickled herring.

Maybe Dad wouldn't take them. He might refuse to let Sol drive them there in Aunt Gussie's big, fancy car.

But when Sol pulled the Pierce Arrow up to the curb, Dad was already waiting there in the snow. He climbed into the car with a face full of things to do and places to go.

"Lawndale?" Sol grunted from the front seat.

"No," Dad said, dusting off his hat.

Before Rudy even felt his eyes light up, his father added, "Take us to the South State Street Jail."

"The *jail?*" Rudy said.

"Yes. We're going to see Nathaniel Levitsky."

✢ ✢ ✢

Chapter Seven

*I*n the midst of all the other buildings, decorated with lights and garlands and as much sparkle as any shop owner could afford, the police station looked even gloomier than it probably did normally.

"They could at least hang a wreath on the door," Hildy Helen whispered to her brothers as they followed Dad inside.

"Yeah, but Nathaniel doesn't notice," Rudy whispered back. "What does he know about Christmas decorations? He's Jewish."

Mr. Hutchinson frowned. "Now, remember, all of you," he murmured. "I had to get special permission to bring you with me, so no shenanigans. And don't forget—anything Nathaniel tells us is private."

When they entered a cold, gray room, Rudy stopped short. There was Nathaniel Levitsky sitting at a table in the center, slumped in a chair with his hands buried in his lap. *Yeah, he looks Jewish, all right,* Rudy thought. *But he's barely older than me!*

Nathaniel was on the small side for 15. He had none of the thickness of his parents or his sister. In fact, Rudy would never have picked him out in a line-up as Isabel's brother. Rudy would have been hard-put to find a comical feature to exaggerate for a caricature; Nathaniel had soft brown eyes and a finely chiseled

66

face. And right now that face was pinched with fear.

"He's a fish," Little Al whispered as Dad crossed the room to introduce himself.

"What do you mean, a fish?" Hildy Helen whispered back.

"Somebody thrown in jail for the first time. He's never been in before. You can tell by his eyes."

By now Dad was sitting at the table with Nathaniel, and he motioned the children over. Rudy could feel his feet dragging, and the chairs seemed to make a deafening noise as they scraped them back to sit down.

"Are they treating you all right?" Dad said to Nathaniel.

"Sure," Nathaniel said. "They treat me like a criminal, but it's not so bad."

His voice had none of Uriah's Polish accent. It was soft, especially next to the snappish voices of the policemen talking in the hall, and intelligent-sounding.

"You think this is bad," Little Al said. "They say if you go up the river, it's twice what this is."

"Al, Nathaniel is not going to prison. We're here to make sure of that." Dad said.

"'Course not," Al said. He lowered his voice. "But take some advice—don't beat the guards in cards. Let 'em win, and they'll put in a good word for you."

Nathaniel's eyes flickered.

"Yeah, I done some time," Al said. He patted Nathaniel on the shoulder.

Rudy wanted to give Little Al a sharp jab with his elbow. He was making friends with the kid! Good grief!

"But you see that Al is a free man," Dad said, smiling at Nathaniel. "And I represented him. That should give you some hope."

Nathaniel looked down at his lap.

"Relax, son," Dad said. "There's no need for you to be

ashamed. You've been given a bum rap."

You don't know that! Rudy wanted to shout.

Nathaniel, however, brightened a little. He sat up in his chair and put his hands on the table. They were linked together at the wrists with handcuffs.

Rudy's eyes riveted to them, and he couldn't pry them away. Handcuffs. Nobody had said anything about handcuffs. It made Rudy suddenly feel as if he couldn't breathe.

"Tell me what happened the day Victor Vedoli was shot," Dad said.

Little Al twitched, Rudy looked at him, but he was watching Nathaniel closely.

"Didn't my father tell you?" Nathaniel said.

"He did," Dad said. "I'd just like to hear it from you."

What do you want to bet it's different? Rudy thought. *Maybe then Dad will give up this stupid case and we can go back home.* But as Nathaniel told his story, it was exactly as Uriah Levitsky had spun it out for them the day before. Only Nathaniel told it with a tremble in his voice that set Rudy's stomach churning.

As Dad began to ask Nathaniel questions, Little Al whispered to Rudy, "He must be a tough guy on the inside, 'cause he sure isn't on the outside. And I know one thing—"

Dad's voice grew louder. "I'm going to do all I can to represent you fairly, Nathaniel. I'm going to try to see that justice is done."

"Thank you, sir," Nathaniel said, and once again Rudy was surprised at how educated he sounded. Was he one of those yeshiva students, whatever they were?

Dad stood up and put his notebook into his pocket, and the children hurriedly scraped their chairs back, too.

I've never been so glad to get out of a place, Rudy thought. *This joint gives me the heebie-jeebies.*

"One more thing," Dad said. "What, if anything, can I do for you right now to make all of this easier?"

"There is one thing," Nathaniel said. "Could you please look after my sister? I think my mother and father are so upset, they aren't paying much attention to her. I'm the only one she really trusts anyway."

"Why's that?" Hildy Helen said.

Rudy kept back a groan. Could they just stop with the questions and get out of here?

"My parents don't really listen to her and she doesn't have many friends. She gets teased a lot," Nathaniel said. "It's made her skittish."

"Yeah, nothin' worse than people razzin' yer sister," Little Al said. He jerked his head toward Hildy Helen. "I gotta take care of that kinda thing all the time."

"Little Al, that gives me an idea," Dad said. "I think you and Hildy Helen and Rudy are just the people to keep an eye on Isabel."

If the rest of the Hutchinsons had thought Rudy pouted on the way to the jail, they hadn't seen anything like the kind of sulking that occurred on the way back. When Little Al whispered to Rudy, "I know Nathaniel couldn't a shot Vic Vedoli. Vic's one of the toughest, and Nathaniel, he ain't," Rudy just grunted and turned toward the window.

When he got home, Rudy had an urge to go upstairs and draw a decidedly ugly picture of his father promising Rudy's hand to Isabel in marriage. But they had the pageant to get ready for.

The three children had to get into their costumes and get to school an hour before the pageant was scheduled to start. And there was Hildy Helen to think about.

"Let me see that ankle," Aunt Gussie said as they were pulling on their coats. Rudy noticed that Al's silky pants looked suspiciously like Oxford bags.

"It's fine, Aunt Gussie, I promise," Hildy Helen said. "In fact, it feels so good, I want to walk to the school to get my muscles warmed up."

"You'll do no such thing."

"But why should Sol make two trips? It'll help me, Aunt Gussie, honest it will. I have to get the muscles working. And besides, remember I rested it this afternoon?"

Aunt Gussie looked doubtful, and Hildy Helen's eyes started to fill again.

"I tell you what, Miss Gustavio," Little Al said. "If Hildy Helen gets tired walkin' down to the school, I'll carry her."

"You will not!" Hildy Helen said.

"Then you won't go," Aunt Gussie said.

Hildy Helen held up her arms to Little Al without a moment's hesitation, and even Aunt Gussie had to laugh.

"Go on then, all three of you," she said. "We'll be along later. And buckle up those galoshes, Hildegarde. I don't care what the fashion is, you will not walk down the street with the fool things flapping open."

For once, Hildy Helen didn't protest that Bridget wore hers that way. One more argument and Rudy knew she'd spend the rest of the evening in her room, pageant or no pageant.

It had stopped snowing as they started off, but it was colder now that darkness had fallen, and the sidewalk was icy. It was a good thing Aunt Gussie hadn't noticed just how slick it was. They paused at the corner, out of sight of Aunt Gussie's house, so Hildy Helen could unfasten her galoshes and Little Al could take off his hat.

"What did you put on your hair?" Rudy said, staring at the shine on Little Al's head.

"Brilliantine," he said, cocking a half smile. "I think it makes me look swell, don't you?"

"It doesn't make you smell swell," Rudy said. He didn't add that it gave off a worse aroma than Hildy Helen's witch hazel.

"And I gotta look swell," Al said, "seein's how I'm right on the front row."

"You're as big a ham as I am," Hildy Helen said. "We're both gonna be stars tonight. You, too, Rudy."

"Nah," Rudy said, and he truly didn't care to be. Give him a pen and a sketch pad and he was happy. Two stars in the family were enough.

He looked around now as they picked their way around patches of ice. There was always something that would be fun to draw. Maybe he'd do a sketch of the way the snow collected in little piles on the sidewalk and made patterns as the wind blew. Or perhaps he'd do one of the lonely way the empty lots looked, all heaped with snow where elegant homes used to be.

"How come they just tore them down? Why didn't they sell them?" Rudy had asked Aunt Gussie once.

"To avoid taxes," she said. "It's all about money for them. But not for me."

"Yer limpin', Hildy Helen," Little Al said suddenly. "Come on, get on my back."

"I'll feel silly!"

"You'll feel even sillier if you fall on your face on the stage," Rudy said.

Hildy Helen cocked her head at him. "You sounded like Dad just then," she said.

"Did not!"

"Come on, shake a leg," Little Al said. "We gotta get goin'. If I don't show on time, Miss Dollface is liable to give Maury my part."

"Climb on!" Rudy said.

He hoisted Hildy Helen up onto Little Al's back, and the two took off in tandem with Rudy leading the way.

"You scout for ice patches, Rudy," Little Al said.

"It's hard to see them," he said over his shoulder. "The snow's covered them up."

"Never mind, then," Little Al said. "I got a good feel for that kinda thing."

No sooner were the words out of his mouth, than Rudy heard a squeal. When he turned around, both Little Al and Hildy Helen were sprawled on the sidewalk, legs sticking up in four different directions.

"Jeepers!" Rudy cried.

"I'm all right," Hildy Helen said. She untangled herself from Little Al and stood up.

"Your ankle's all right?" Rudy said.

"It's fine. I don't think Little Al is though."

Rudy looked down to see Al lying flat on his back in the snow.

"Look at that," Rudy said. "Your hair didn't even get messed up!"

"That's good," Little Al said. He shook off the snow and scrambled up, running his hand down the back of his head.

"I can't say the same for your costume," Hildy Helen said.

"What?" Little Al said. "Did it rip?"

Hildy Helen was examining his backside. "No, but the seat of your pants is soaked clean through. It looks like you had an accident!"

"Naw!" Little Al said.

"What in glory is wrong this time?"

They looked up to see Officer O'Dell striding toward them, the collar of his heavy brown jacket pulled up around his ears and his hands shoved into his pockets. His poor nose looked like a piece of raw meat from the cold.

"Nothing," Rudy said.

"Except we have to get to the school fast," Hildy Helen said. "And I'm *not* getting on Little Al's back again."

"Will mine do, lassie?" Officer O'Dell said.

Before Hildy Helen could answer, the big policeman had scooped her up and was headed toward Felthensal. Rudy gave a hoot and went off after them.

"You coming, Al?" he called back.

"I'm comin." Little Al said. His voice was disgruntled. "Don't you dare say a word about this to anybody, or there won't be no end to the razzin'."

"You got my word," Rudy said. "I'll walk in behind you so nobody'll see."

They entered the assembly hall like two pieces of bologna stuck together, but there was no need.

Miss Tibbs honed right in on Hildy Helen.

"Does it still hurt?" she said.

"No!" Hildy Helen said.

"Let me see that ankle."

No amount of protesting would change Miss Tibbs's mind. The galoshes came off, and the ankle was produced. Miss Tibbs studied it until Rudy thought she was going to ask for a microscope next.

"The swelling has gone down some," she said. "It doesn't look quite as bruised."

"It does to me."

Rudy didn't know when Dorothea had joined them. Long enough to see the black and blue blotches on Hildy's ankle anyway.

"I don't think she should dance on that," Dorothea said. "I don't know who your teacher is, but mine would never let a dancer perform on an injury like that."

"Well, this teacher thinks it's just fine," Miss Tibbs said. "Put your shoe back on Hildy Helen, and get ready."

"She's going to be terrible. She's going to smell up the whole stage!" Dorothea said.

Little Al gave a deep bow as Dorothea stomped off. Hildy Helen grinned at Rudy.

"I think Miss Tibbs did that because Dorothea is such a terrible dancer," she whispered.

"See?" Rudy whispered back. "When people are un-Christian, they get punished, it's as simple as that. They get what they deserve."

From the corner of the assembly hall there was a sudden bellow, and they both jumped.

"It's just Maury, yelling as usual," Hildy Helen said.

"Doesn't it kind of remind you of a cow back in Shelbyville?"

"Only that one we knocked over when she was sleeping," Hildy Helen said. Her eyes were sparkling again. "Everything's gonna be all right, Rudy. I get to dance!"

"But my sister doesn't!" a voice bellowed at them. "And somebody's gonna pay for that."

Maury was vaulting across the assembly hall seats, his eyes boring into the Hutchinson twins. From out of nowhere, Little Al reappeared, hands on hips.

"Like who?" he said.

Maury didn't answer. He was trying to catch his breath. Grinning, Little Al turned away from Maury and toward Hildy Helen and Rudy.

"Looks like it's gonna be you!" Maury cried. "Hey, Miss Tibbs!"

"Maury, lower your voice," Miss Tibbs said from the stage. "It's time to get to your places. Come on, now."

"But look at him. Look at Alonzo!" Maury said, pointing at Little Al's pants.

Little Al had by now recovered himself and had moved his hands to cover his backside. Rudy hurried up behind him and resumed his place as the second piece of bologna.

But the trick didn't fool the sharp-eyed Miss Tibbs. She sighed and crooked her finger at them. "Up here, both of you," she said.

Slowly they made their way up to the stage. Rudy thought maybe if they took their time, Little Al's pants would dry off by the time they got up there.

"What is it now?" Miss Tibbs said. But she didn't need an answer. Her eyes went right to Little Al's knees. "What are those wet spots?" she said.

Little Al looked down in surprise. "There, too?" he said.

"Well, where else?" Miss Tibbs said.

"Right there on his ugly backside!" Maury hollered.

Everyone who had gathered on the risers set up a howl that took three rounds of hand-clapping from Miss Tibbs to stop. Even then, they had to slap their hands over their mouths to smother their laughter.

"Let me see, Al," Miss Tibbs said. She turned Little Al with a jerk and sighed from the toes of her patent leather pumps. "Oh, for crying out loud," she said. "You're going to have to stand on the back row now, Al."

"Aw, say it ain't so, Miss Dollface!" Little Al said.

"Well, I'm certainly not going to have you in front with a soaking wet costume. You can do your part from up there."

Little Al scowled, but he didn't say a word. The only sound was a snicker from behind them.

"What was that, Maury?" Miss Tibbs said.

"Nothin," Maury said. "He just deserves it, is all."

"He isn't the only one. I think since you're getting such a big kick out of all of this, you can jolly well stand up there, too. Both of you—to the back row."

To Rudy's surprise, Maury didn't squall. He just flung himself into the second row, whispered to George and Clark, and then shoved several people out of the way to get to the top. Little Al was already there, trying to look tall so he would still stand out in the crowd.

Don't worry, Little Al, Rudy thought. *You look swell, even from there.*

Then Rudy craned his neck to see Hildy Helen taking her place backstage. She was standing poised in the wings while the audience filtered in from outside. She already looked like a snowflake.

Jesus is gonna help you, Hildy, Rudy thought. *After all, He's on* our *side.*

The assembly hall filled quickly with proud parents, and although Miss Tibbs had told them not to look out at the crowd, Rudy spotted Dad, Aunt Gussie, Bridget, Quintonia, and Sol all sitting in the second row, right in the center. He also thought he saw his father smile and wink at Miss Tibbs when she came onstage.

That, he decided, had to be his imagination.

Then suddenly it was time to begin. Miss Tibbs nodded to Miss Erwin, who started plunking out the music.

Right from the start, Rudy could feel it going well—better than at any rehearsal. Somehow the audience made them all stand up straighter and try harder and sing better. Even from the top row, Little Al was in rare form. Rudy could almost feel Dad and Aunt Gussie smiling and nudging each other.

When it was time for the snowflake dance, Rudy didn't even hold his breath. The minute he saw Hildy Helen float out from the wings, he knew the audience was making her try harder, too. And she looked better than she ever had. Rudy reminded himself to draw her when he got home—not a funny drawing, but something where she was part actual snowflake and part Hildy Helen. He was concentrating so hard on that, he almost missed her twirl. He didn't, though, because as she spun into it, the audience gave an appreciative gasp. Hildy's face shone as it turned Rudy's way, and he felt a strange surge inside.

And then, abruptly, Hildy disappeared. Rudy heard a thud,

louder even than the snowflake music plunking from Miss Erwin's piano, and he stretched to see.

It was his turn to gasp. Hildy Helen was lying on the floor.

✝ ✦ ✝

Chapter Eight

A murmur started through the audience. Before it got to the back of the assembly hall, Hildy Helen scrambled up. Rudy couldn't see her face as she went into her snowflake leap, but from the way her arms stuck stiffly into the air, he knew she was hurt.

Behind her, the other dancers fumbled in confusion with their steps, looking as if they hadn't a clue as to where they were sup-posed to be in the dance. All of them struggled to catch up—except Dorothea. With a leap of her own, she bounded to the front next to Hildy Helen, in perfect step with the music. The other snowflakes flailed for a moment or two longer and finally fell into sync with her.

Hildy Helen, too, bravely continued to twirl and leap. To Rudy she still looked like the best snippet of snow out there. But he knew she didn't think so. When she turned into her final twirl, he saw tears shining in her eyes. And when the song ended, she was the first to bow and dance off the stage. Dorothea took more than enough bows for the both of them.

The audience applauded wildly. Rudy looked up at Little Al. His face was scarlet, and his eyes were drilling into the side of Maury's face. Rudy, too, glared at Maury—and then a thought came. *It couldn't have been Maury who tripped her this time*, he thought. *Even he couldn't do it from the back row!*

When the pageant was over, it was obvious Miss Tibbs didn't think so either. Rudy got backstage as soon as he could. He found Miss Tibbs, with tears in her own eyes, sitting on the floor next to a swollen-eyed Hildy Helen.

"It's my fault," she was saying when Rudy got to them. "I shouldn't have let you dance."

"Is she all right?" It was Dad, elbowing his way through the other parents and their kids with Aunt Gussie right behind him.

"Her ankle just gave out as far as I could tell," Miss Tibbs said. "I'm so sorry, Jim. I used bad judgment."

There was no mistaking it this time. Dad did pass his hand lightly over Miss Tibbs' shoulder. But this was no time to think about that. Aunt Gussie had already ordered Sol to bring the car around and had sent Bridget to call for Dr. Kennedy to meet them at the house. Dad went back and forth between comforting Miss Tibbs, who insisted on coming with them, and fussing over Hildy Helen. Rudy just stood there feeling miserable until Quintonia finally came in to tell them that the car was ready. Dad picked up Hildy Helen and carried her out.

They were all inside the house on Prairie Avenue a half hour later, bending with Dr. Kennedy over Hildy Helen in the parlor, when Bridget came quietly up to Rudy and said, "Have you seen Little Al?"

Rudy jumped. In all the concern over Hildy Helen, Rudy hadn't even missed Al. An image of his Italian brother beating the stuffing out of Maury Worthington in some dark alley flashed across his mind.

"No," he whispered, "but I'll go look for him. Don't tell Dad, okay?"

"Just go," Bridget whispered. "Keep that boy out of trouble!"

Rudy hadn't taken off his coat yet, so he hurried right out the front door. Only when he was at the end of the front walk, and his hands were like claws at his sides, did he realize he'd left his gloves in the Pierce Arrow. He didn't want to risk going back into the house to ask for the keys. If Dad knew what he was up to, that would be the end of finding Little Al before he got into real trouble with Aunt Gussie.

It was starting to snow again, and the flakes were falling sideways in the wind. Rudy's muffler flew out behind him as he shoved his hands into his pockets and leaned into the storm.

Jesus, please let him still be at the school, he prayed. *You'll help me find him. I know You will.*

He didn't have a chance to add *because I'm on Your side* before his right foot shot out from under him, and he had to grope at the air to keep his balance. Now that it was snowing again, it was harder than ever to see the icy patches on the sidewalk. He stepped off the concrete and waded through the deepening drifts. It was slower going, but if he fell on his tail, he might not get there at all.

I sure wish Officer O'Dell would show up, he thought. But their policeman friend had long since gone off duty, and the nighttime officers only cruised through the neighborhood once every hour or two. He was going to have to check out the school alone.

By the time he got to Felthensal, the building was dark and the doors were locked. Rudy stuffed his now frozen claws into his pockets and stood against a light pole to think.

Where would he be? Rudy asked himself. Little Al had said just that afternoon that if Hildy Helen didn't get to dance, he had a plan for getting Maury Worthington. What had happened was nearly as bad—maybe worse. He'd never in his whole life seen Hildy Helen look embarrassed. She flipped her brown bob of hair at everything. She never seemed to care what other people thought. But that dance had been important to her, and she'd fallen down in front of everyone.

Little Al was definitely getting revenge on Maury. The question was *where?*

Maury's house? Rudy wondered. *I don't even know where Maury lives. I don't even know who to ask. The only person I know who would even care would be Miss Tibbs.*

And Miss Tibbs was right there at Aunt Gussie's. He'd have to go back. The trick would be to get Maury's address from her and leave the house again without Dad catching him.

Jesus, You'll help me, right? Rudy prayed as he moved away from the light pole.

He stepped to the curb and looked down the street. A car had appeared so suddenly, Rudy had the crazy thought that Jesus was probably driving it.

Whoever this is probably hasn't seen Little Al, Rudy thought. *But it won't hurt to ask.*

He raised his hand to flag down the car, but it was already pulling up to the curb beside him. The window on the passenger side rolled down, and Rudy saw a neatly creased fedora and the fur collar of an overcoat.

"Hey, kid," said its wearer. "Come over here."

Something in the man's surly voice sent a chill colder than the winter night itself up Rudy's spine. He could almost hear Officer O'Dell warning him: *Stay out of bad neighborhoods.*

But this is my *neighborhood*, Rudy thought. *I can handle my own street!*

He forced himself to take on a voice he hoped sounded like Al Capone's—at least Little Al's. "What for?" he said to the man in the car.

"So you can hear what I gotta say!" the man said. His voice was gruff with annoyance, and he turned to the driver.

Rudy backed up and started down the sidewalk, his feet slipping and sliding in the snow. The car door flew open and the fur-collared man stepped out, still grumbling. "You make me get out in the snow, you'll make me mad," he barked at Rudy. "And you don't wanna make me mad."

Rudy's first thought was to run, but his next step sent his foot veering crazily to the left. *This is my neighborhood*, Rudy thought. *Jesus is on my side!*

He dug his hands deeper into his pockets and stood still. The man careened down the sidewalk and stopped in front of him. He had his bullet-shaped head and face half hidden under his hat, and there was no way to tell who he was. He, on the other hand, seemed to recognize Rudy right away.

"Well, well, well!" he said. "Isn't this a stroke of luck? This must be my Christmas present!"

Rudy's stomach churned, but he curled his lip at the man. "Whatta ya mean by that?" he said.

"Just what I said. I got the Little Hutchie wrapped up and practically dropped in my lap!"

It was time, Rudy decided, to trust his instincts and run like crazy, ice or no ice. Even as the man reached out a gloved hand, Rudy took a step backward, but he wasn't fast enough. The man grabbed his arm, swung him around, and pinned both arms behind Rudy's back. Rudy tried to pull away, but he couldn't break free. The man's grip was like a vise, even when he let go with one hand.

The reason why was immediately apparent. Rudy felt something hard and cold press against the back of his neck. He wasn't sure—he hadn't had much experience with these things the way Little Al had—but he thought it might be a gun. He stopped struggling.

"I like a Christmas gift like this," the man said. "Let's go put you under my tree."

Rudy had no choice but to go. The man pushed Rudy ahead of him and moved him toward the waiting car. Rudy was sure he was going to throw up. He couldn't think enough to even consider how to get away. He couldn't even pray.

And suddenly there was no need to. Behind him, Bullet-Head reared backward, his feet flying out to either side. He fell heavily to the sidewalk with Rudy on top of him.

It took a surprised moment for Rudy to realize the man's arms had sprung apart. He rolled away into the snow beside the sidewalk.

You're free! his mind screamed at him. *Get up and run!* But before he could obey his own thoughts, another hand grabbed his arm. Rudy gave a yank, but a voice close to his ear whispered, "It's me, ya dope! Let's go!"

Rudy's face broke into a grin, and he crawled to his feet. With Bullet-Head still moaning on the sidewalk, he ran like a high-stepping horse through the snow after Little Al.

Al led him over an ice-cold iron gate that locked out the world from an empty lot. The remains of a fireplace still stood at its edge, and Little Al tore toward it with Rudy following at a clumsy gallop. They both hurled themselves behind it and breathed out frosty air like a pair of steam engines.

Slowly, a black form rose from the sidewalk and grabbed for its hat and, to the boys' relief, stumbled toward the waiting car. With an angry puff of exhaust, the car pulled away from the curb and sped off down Prairie Avenue.

Eyes wide, Rudy turned to Al. "Where've you been?" Rudy demanded. "I been looking all over for you!"

"I went lookin' for Maury, of course."

"Did you find him?"

Al shook his head and, peeking out from behind the fireplace one more time, stood up and brushed the snow off his silk pants.

"These aren't the best thing to be wearin' around in the snow," he said. "I'm about to freeze my backside."

"My hands are already frozen," Rudy said. "I can't even feel them anymore."

"We gotta go home," Little Al said.

"You giving up on getting Maury?"

"Says you!" Little Al's eyes gleamed as they passed under a streetlight. "I just gotta find out where he lives."

"Ask Miss Tibbs," Rudy said. "She's at our house."

"I know. I was on my way there when I seen you was in trouble."

"I thought I was a goner," Rudy said. The sick feeling returned to his stomach. "I never been that close to dyin' before."

"Nah, they wouldn't a killed ya," Little Al said. "Not for a while anyway." He waved that off. "Besides, I saved ya."

"You did not save me either!" Rudy said. "That fella fell down on the ice!"

"Only because I put it there."

"Aw, come on, Al!" Rudy said. "You can't take the credit for that. The whole sidewalk is icy."

"But I made it icy in just the right spot."

Little Al stopped and leaned over, picking up a thick slice of ice the size of a dinner plate. "It gets like this over the puddles," he said. "I just picked one up and threw it in front of him. He was down before he even knew what happened."

Rudy stared at him as they walked on toward home. Little Al never stopped amazing him.

"So—" Little Al said, as if it had been a normal day's work. "How are we gonna get the address from Miss Tibbs?"

"Are you sure we need to do that?" Rudy said. Now that he'd found Little Al, he wasn't so sure he wanted to go out again tonight.

"Whatta you sayin?" Little Al said. "We gotta get even for Hildy Helen."

"But it couldn't have been Maury this time," Rudy said. "He

was standing on the back row with you. How could he trip her from up there?"

"It don't matter," Little Al said, setting his jaw. "I warned him—"

"All right, so what if we wait and talk to Hildy Helen—you know, find out what happened from her."

Little Al looked at him admiringly. "You gotta point, Rudolpho," he said. "We ain't had her alone since it happened. I bet Miss Gustavio sent for the doctor."

"Of course," Rudy said.

Little Al nodded thoughtfully. "All right. We wait 'til we talk to her. Then we come up with a plan. No, I come up with a plan. You got enough trouble as it is."

"Me?" Rudy said. "Seems like you're in it with me now. You have to help keep an eye on that Isabel girl, too."

"Yeah, but it's for Nathaniel. It's the least we can do."

Rudy stared at him. "What are *you* talkin' about?" he said.

"I don't think he coulda done it, Rudolpho," Al said. "I knew Vic Vedoli. But forget that for now. My question is, are we gonna fill Mr. Hutchie in on this?"

"You mean about Maury?" Rudy said.

"No, ya dope! About you practically gettin' plugged right here on Prairie Avenue."

"Oh," Rudy said. He rubbed the back of his neck where the gun had pressed. "We probably oughtta."

"I vote no," Little Al said. "We tell him about this, and he ain't never gonna let us out after dark again 'til we're about 30 years old—and that's old!"

Rudy shivered a little. "But shouldn't that fella be arrested or something?"

"You're afraid he's gonna come after ya again, aren't ya?" Little Al said.

"Yeah," Rudy said. He straightened his glasses.

"Hey, Rudolpho." Little Al punched him playfully on the arm. "You don't gotta worry about it. I'm always here to protect ya."

Rudy hunched up his shoulders against the cold and sort of wagged his head. Little Al laughed and plunged on through the snow.

Rudy had to admit, he liked having Little Al's protection.

✝ ✝ ✝

Chapter Nine

*T*here was no getting information out of Hildy Helen that night. Dr. Kennedy had given her a sedative, and she was snoring when Rudy and Little Al slipped into her room and stood looking down at her.

"She sounds like a train," Little Al whispered.

Rudy nodded absently. He was busy looking at her face, which bore the telltale trails of tears. They were so unfamiliar to him, he couldn't take his eyes off them, and in his mind he was drawing them, long and sad and painful.

"She really wanted to dance good tonight," he said.

"Don't I know it," Little Al said. "That's why we gotta get that Maury Worthington."

"I don't know. We were going to talk to Hildy first," Rudy said slowly.

"Who knows when she'll wake up. And we gotta start now. Here's the plan."

Instead of leaning in intently and soaking up Al's plan the way he usually did, Rudy listened with only half his mind, while the other half wished Al would stuff his mouth full of ravioli and hush up. This sounded like trouble—trouble Rudy couldn't afford to get into. But, still, if a person wasn't a Christian, didn't he deserve to be punished for the lousy things he did?

"You got it?" Little Al said.

"What?"

"What you're supposed to do!"

"Uh, no."

Little Al shook his head. "You artists. You sure drift off a lot. You go to Mr. Hutchie and keep him busy while I hit up Miss Dollface for Maury's address. Now you got it?"

Dad and Miss Tibbs were in the library, deep in conversation. When the boys came in, the two adults looked startled, as if they'd forgotten Rudy and Al were even in the house. Dad had a funny expression on his face. As far as Rudy was concerned, he looked a lot like a sick dog.

Little Al jabbed Rudy with his elbow. "Do it!" he hissed out of the side of his mouth.

"Dad?" Rudy said.

Dad dragged his eyes from Miss Tibbs's face to Rudy's. "Hmm?" he said.

"Um, can I talk to you?"

Dad jumped. "Of course!" he said, with more enthusiasm than Rudy thought necessary. "Effa—uh—Miss Tibbs, would you excuse us?"

"I really need to be going anyway," she said. Her cheeks were a pair of blotches as she stood up and fumbled for her coat.

"Then I'll see ya to the door, Miss Dollface!" Little Al said. He held out his arm, and she linked hers through it. Rudy could hear him launching into his part of the plan even as the library door closed. He himself looked lamely at his father.

"I'm glad you came down," Dad said. "There was something I wanted to discuss with you, too."

Rudy plastered on a big grin. "Swell, Dad! What is it?"

If Dad noticed that Rudy was acting like an idiot, he didn't show it. He took on his business face again and folded his hands on the table. "Tomorrow I'm going to take you and Little Al to the Levitskys."

"Again?" Rudy said.

"They have invited us to join them for their holiday celebration."

"But they're Jewish!"

"Rudy, I think we have established that," Dad said, his voice dry. "Tomorrow is the first day of Hanukkah. They've asked us to join them for the ceremony."

"But that isn't part of working on Nathaniel's case. Why do I have to go?"

"Because this will give you a chance to honor our promise to keep an eye on Isabel."

That was your promise, not mine! Rudy thought. *Jesus, how come Dad doesn't see these Jewish people aren't on Your side? Why are we wasting time helping them? What about Hildy Helen?*

Jesus, however, didn't seem to be speaking to his father at the moment. "Now, what was it you wanted to talk about?" Dad said.

Mercifully the door opened then, and Little Al poked his head in and said, "Miss Dollface says good-bye."

"Oh!" Dad said and rushed to the front door.

Little Al gave Rudy a shove toward the stairs. "That lady oughtta be in the mob," he whispered. "She wouldn't give me the goods for nothin'."

"You didn't get Maury's address, huh?" Rudy said.

Little Al stopped at the top of the steps. "You sound like you're kinda glad," he said.

Rudy was saved from having to answer by a particularly loud snore from Hildy Helen's end of the hall.

"The train's leaving," he said, grinning.

Little Al grunted. "You can be yella about this if you want to,

Rudolpho, but I'm gettin' back at Maury Worthington if it's the last thing I do."

Then he swaggered on into their room. Rudy went into Hildy Helen's. He didn't want to talk about this with Little Al anymore, and for some reason, he wanted to be right next to Hildy Helen.

The snow gave off a soft light against the window, so Rudy could see enough to pile some quilts on the floor next to the bed and curl up on them.

We used to do this when we were kids, he thought. Any time either one of them was sick, the other would sleep on the floor next to the bed until the other twin was better. Neither one of them ever said it, but Rudy was pretty sure Hildy Helen believed what he did: that they would always get better if the other one was there.

What if something ever did *happen to Hildy Helen?* he thought suddenly. *Is a sprained ankle fatal? Could there be— what do you call them—"complicateds" or something?*

Suddenly it was cold and lonely on the floor, and Rudy scooted closer to the bed. Above him, Hildy snored him to sleep.

It was Hildy Helen who woke him up, too, the minute the sun started to sparkle on the ice crystals at the window. When Rudy opened his eyes, she was leaning out from the bed, her nose almost touching his.

"Are you awake?" she said.

"I am now."

"Then get up here. I want to talk to you."

Rudy scrambled gratefully into the bed with her, shivering from the early-morning cold. Aunt Gussie always kept the furnace turned down low at night. She said it wasn't healthy to sleep with hot air blasting you. Rudy thought they must be the healthiest people in the world.

"You and Little Al have to do something, Rudy," Hildy Helen said. "I know it was Maury and them who made me fall."

"But Maury was on the top row, and George and them were on the second. They'd have to have legs like a giraffe to trip you."

"Nobody tripped me. And my ankle didn't give out either. It felt just the way it did when Little Al and I slipped on the ice. I was dancing the best I ever had, and all of a sudden my feet just weren't under me anymore."

"I don't get it," Rudy said.

"There was something on the stage. It was slippery. It never felt like that before."

Rudy had to nod, and then another thought crept in. "You know what else?" he said. "The other dancers were all confused when you fell, but Dorothea just kept dancing."

"Like she knew it was going to happen!" Hildy Helen said. "See? I told you! You didn't hear all those people backstage, Rudy, telling her she'd saved the day." She clenched her fists. "Ooh, she makes me so mad! That's why I want you and Little Al to find out exactly who did it and what they did—and get them!"

For about the 50th time in the last two days, tears sprang into Hildy's eyes, and for Rudy it was one time too many. He felt like maybe getting Maury Worthington wasn't such a bad idea after all. It didn't settle down peacefully inside him the way a good idea did, but he turned his head from that.

"All right," he said, throwing back the covers. "Me and Little Al will start right away. All we have to do is find out where Maury lives and go over there and—"

"I don't think you goin' nowhere, boy," Quintonia said from the doorway. She was carrying a tray with cinnamon smells wafting from it, which she set on Hildy's bedside table. "Your daddy just tol' me to tell you not to leave this house today and to be ready when he gets home from his office. You goin' somewhere over Lawndale way, is what he said."

Rudy looked at Hildy Helen and rolled his eyes.

"Don't worry, it will happen," Hildy Helen whispered. She

gave her dark bob a toss and said, "Could I please have some butter, Quintonia? I like butter on my cinnamon rolls." The tears
were gone. She was back to being Hildy again—and Rudy was
going to keep it that way.

"Do I get to go to Lawndale, too?" she said as Quintonia put
a glass of freshly squeezed orange juice into her hand.

"You're not steppin' on that ankle today less'n it's over my
dead body," Quintonia said.

"Huh," Rudy said to Hildy. "I'd trade places with you any day."

"I can arrange a broke ankle for you, too, Rudolph,"
Quintonia said.

"I was just leaving," Rudy said.

"Just leavin' this room, not this house, and don't you forget
that."

He certainly didn't. All day while Quintonia was baking
Christmas fruitcakes, Rudy and Little Al looked for ways to slip
out and start the search for the Worthingtons. But Quintonia
seemed to be able to hear their thoughts as they crept toward a
door or window. And as for Aunt Gussie and Bridget, both of them
seemed to be everywhere. When Dad came home in the late afternoon, they'd made absolutely no progress, and Little Al was
restless as a fiddler without a bow.

"Get dressed," Dad said to them. "Your Sunday best. This is
a special occasion."

Rudy heard the phone ring while he was upstairs putting on
his wool tweed knicker suit. It had a matching Windsor cap,
which meant the ensemble itched from head to toe. Little Al
didn't mind dressing up the way Rudy did. In fact, he was in the
bathroom slicking back his hair so it would look just so.

Several seconds later Rudy heard Dad say from the phone in
the library, "Who is this? Who is it!"

Rudy dashed out into the hall and collided with Little Al, already on his way down. By the time they reached the library, Dad

had already replaced the receiver on its candlestick holder, but his face was splotchy with anger.

"What on earth was that about, James?" Aunt Gussie said as she swept in, raw silk rustling.

"From now on, no one is to answer this phone except Aunt Gussie or myself, is that understood?"

Rudy flipped back through his memory. He hadn't played a phone prank in months. This couldn't be about that.

"Why?" Aunt Gussie said. "What is it?"

She turned to the boys and started to shoo them out, but Dad put up his hand. "I think we all need to be aware of this," he said. "The caller wouldn't tell me who he was, but it's easy to guess. He said if I don't give up the Levitsky case, there's going to be trouble."

"It didn't take a fortune-teller to foresee that," Aunt Gussie said. "What are you going to do?"

Rudy allowed himself to hope, but of course Dad shook his head.

"I'm not giving up the case, if that's what you mean."

"I would never even suggest it," Aunt Gussie said. "What would be the point? You have your mind set on representing Nathaniel Levitsky. But what about this 'trouble' that's supposed to occur if you keep on?"

Dad reached for the phone again. "I'm going to call the police station and ask for extra protection here in the neighborhood." He paused, receiver in hand, and directed his eyes at Rudy and Little Al in a rare hard look. "And you children are not to leave this house for any reason without an adult. Am I clear?"

"As a bell, Mr. Hutchie," Little Al said cheerfully.

Rudy knew good and well Little Al had no intention of following that warning. He probably had his fingers crossed behind his back this very minute. Rudy's stomach churned, and he did what he always did when his insides started gurgling.

"Fiddlesticks!" he said. "Now we can't go to Lawndale tonight. Shucks!"

Dad ignored him and picked up the phone. "I'm going to call for a taxi, too. I want Sol to stay here—inside the house, with you women."

Rudy sighed. When he couldn't distract his father with a joke, he might as well quit. Dad was seeing through a tunnel right now, and there was no pulling him out of it.

"That was a big sigh, Rudy," Dad said without looking at him. "Don't worry—none of this is going to ruin our Christmas."

Rudy wasn't at all sure of that as they climbed glumly into the taxi and headed for Lawndale. While he knew Little Al was scheming to get out of the house to look for Maury tomorrow, Rudy was sulking about the evening ahead.

How am I supposed to entertain some girl I don't even know, he thought, *while a bunch of adults perform some dull ceremony for a religion God doesn't even like? What's happened to all our Christmas plans?*

But Rudy was surprised to find the grocery festive when they entered the Levitskys' store. As Mrs. Levitsky showed them upstairs to the family's apartment, she actually turned her straight-line mouth up into a smile. Rudy noticed that she had shed her meat-smeared apron and put on a taffeta dress that scraped and rustled when she walked.

In the living room, which smelled of furniture polish, there was a pile of gaily-wrapped presents and a gleaming table groaning with food. Rudy quickly scanned it for pickled herring, but there was no fish in sight, and he had to admit that most of it smelled good enough to actually eat.

"The sun is setting, Papa," someone said.

Isabel was standing at the window, her nose practically pressed to the glass. She wore a brown velvet dress Rudy knew Hildy Helen would never be caught dead in, but her eyes were shining the way Hildy's did when she was looking forward to something.

She's still pretty funny looking, though, Rudy thought. *And I'm supposed to* watch *her?*

"It will be dark soon," Isabel said insistently.

"It will be dark soon, she says!" Uriah cried. "Such a thing to say! Don't I know it will be dark soon?"

Isabel's head drooped, and she turned back to the window.

"What's so swell about it getting dark?" Little Al said. He stuck out his hand. "I'm Alonzo Delgado Hutchinson," he said. "Pleased to meet you."

Uriah grasped Little Al's hands in both of his, just as he'd done with Dad, and he smiled through his beard. "The questions!" he said. "Always the questions with you boys. My Nathaniel, he always has a question." His eyes misted over as he let go of Little Al's hands. "I know what it is about getting dark, all right. When it is dark, we light the menorah."

He waved his hand toward a brass candleholder that held nine candles, one in the middle and four on each side. The branches that held the side candles swooped up in four half circles from the base. Rudy had never seen one like it—even amid Aunt Gussie's collection of strange artifacts.

That's because it's a Jewish thing, he decided.

"One candle for each night of Hanukkah!" Isabel said. Her voice rushed out like air from a balloon. "Plus the *shamash.*"

Uriah suddenly hissed through his teeth, and Isabel's thick lips came together as if they'd been slapped. She looked down at her high-top shoes.

"What's a *shamash?*" Little Al said.

"The questions! Always the questions!" Uriah cried, still glaring at his daughter. "The *shamash* is the candle in the center. All the other candles are lit from it. The Hanukkah is the Festival of Lights!"

"May I tell the story, Papa, please?" Isabel said.

"In the old days," Uriah went on, as if Isabel hadn't even spoken, "the Jews were oppressed in Jerusalem by the Seleucids. Yah, when have we not been oppressed? Everyone has tried to destroy the Jewish faith."

Dad nodded sympathetically.

"So, so, so, Judah Maccabees and his four brothers, they triumphed for the Jews over their oppressors—and the Jews reclaimed Jerusalem and, of course, their temple. But the altar and the sanctuary had to be rebuilt and cleansed, because the temple had been used for pagan sacrifices. That meant burning incense and oil—"

"But there wasn't enough oil," Isabel put in. "All the oil had been destroyed by the pagans, except one little bottle that Judah and his brothers found. Only enough for one day—"

"The talking! Always the talking!" Uriah said sharply. "There was only oil enough to create light and cleansing for one day. But, but, *but* that oil, that same oil, lasted for eight days! These humble candles symbolize that miracle—the miracle that can happen when we are willing to die for the right to practice our own faith." Uriah looked at Dad and at Little Al and finally at Rudy. "There is no end to the miracles that God can do. Let us remember that. Come—we celebrate."

"I'm ready! I have the matches, Papa!"

Uriah scowled as he nodded. "The oldest child lights the first candle," he said. "Ah, but it cannot be so tonight. Can you imagine such a thing?"

"Next year," Dad said.

Uriah said nothing. He watched, eyebrows lowered, as Isabel lit first the *shamash* and then the first side candle. The room suddenly seemed flooded with light, though there were only two small flames. As they all stared into it, Uriah began to speak softly in a language Rudy had never heard, even at Hull House. When he finished, he looked up at his wife, and to Rudy's amazement her straight mouth opened into a song. As the notes and the words floated from her, and from Isabel beside her, the candlelight flickered on their faces and made everyone look almost alike. Rudy had to blink to tell them apart.

As soon as they finished, Mrs. Levitsky's mouth went back into its line and Uriah clapped his hands.

"This is a festival!" he said. "Nathaniel would want it to be so." Once again he nodded at his wife, and she hurried over to the table that had been teasing Rudy with its smells ever since he'd walked in.

"What was that language you were talkin'?" Little Al said.

"Hebrew," Isabel muttered.

"Ah, enough!" Uriah barked at her. Then he turned to Little Al and softened his eyes. "What language, you ask? That was Hebrew, the sacred language of the Jew."

"Oh," Little Al said, "like Latin for the Catholics."

"No," Uriah said, shaking his head. "Nothing like that. Nothing like that at all!"

He gave Little Al a pitying look before he held out his arm to the table. "Let me tell you about the food—ah, the food—such food we have at Hanukkah!"

As the boys and Dad heaped their plates, Uriah explained that all the foods reflected the miracle of the oil. There were latkes, which were potato pancakes fried in oil, and doughnut-looking things called *sufganiyot*, which, too, were cooked in oil. Mrs. Levitsky served the latkes with a sweet caramel applesauce, next to the *rugalach*, thick rolled pastries filled with fruit and raisins.

When Rudy and Little Al had helped themselves three times at Mrs. Levitsky's insistence—although she would only let Isabel eat one plateful—she passed around a platter covered with round, flat things wrapped in shiny foil.

"Did you make these, Mrs. L.?" Little Al said.

She nodded.

"Then I know they're gonna be good. But what are they, if you don't mind my askin'?"

Isabel gave a little whimper. *She wants to tell us*, Rudy thought. *Why don't they go ahead and let her before she hurts herself trying to hold it in?*

"Ah, the *gelt*!" Uriah said. "You'll like those, all right. My Nathaniel, he can eat 20, 30 every night of Hanukkah."

Rudy wondered if they could be flattened pickled herring, but Uriah unwrapped one to reveal what looked like a chocolate cookie. "For the children," he said.

Rudy and Little Al unwrapped and wolfed down several. Rudy noticed that Isabel didn't take any, but sat swinging her legs and chewing on her lips.

Either she really has to go to the washroom, Rudy thought, *or there's something else coming up she can't wait for.*

When Uriah sat back in his chair and patted his stomach contentedly, Isabel sat forward in hers and in a voice Rudy could barely hear, she said, "The dreidel now, Papa?"

Uriah gave a sharp nod and waved his hand at her, just as if he'd been swatting away an annoying mosquito. Isabel scrambled from her chair and tore across the room, coming back with her hands full of colored items.

"Put these on," she said to Rudy and Little Al. She held out two headbands with paper flames sticking out the top of them.

"What's this for?" Rudy said.

But Little Al dropped his headband onto his head and grinned. "How do I look?" he said.

"For an Italian, you're a handsome boy," Uriah said. "Just like my Nathaniel. You put me in mind of him—always the questions. Always the laughter."

Rudy shoved his flame onto his head and, feeling idiotic, followed Isabel and Little Al to the floor to sit down. Isabel put what looked like a strange wooden top in front of them. Little Al, of course, picked it up and examined it.

"I know I ain't a great reader," Little Al said, "but these words look like somethin' Greek to me."

"Hebrew," Isabel said. She cut her eyes toward her father, but he was already engrossed in a conversation with Dad. Isabel poked her finger at each side of the top and read: "Nun, gimel, he, shin."

"Numgimel heyshin?" Little Al said. "It's gotta nice ring to it."

"It means 'a great miracle happened there.' "

"Where?" Al said.

"In the temple, dope," Rudy said. "Weren't you listening?"

Little Al grinned. "Nah. I had my eye on them doughnut things."

"Do you want to play?" Isabel said, looking straight at Rudy with her pointy little eyes.

Rudy shrugged, but Little Al said, "Sure!"

Oh, well, Rudy thought. *At least we don't have to think of a way to keep an eye on her.*

It wasn't Rudy's idea of a swell evening, spinning a dumb little top and singing some song over and over. Little Al seemed willing enough to play along, but Rudy quickly grew bored. After about half an hour, when the top spun his way, he snatched it up.

"Little Al!" he said. "Catch!"

Mr. Hutchinson looked up from his conversation. "Boys . . . " he warned in a low voice.

"Don't worry, we won't break it," Rudy said. He tossed the dreidel to Al, who caught it deftly and spun it on his index finger.

"No!" Isabel cried. "That isn't how you play!"

"That's how *we* play," Rudy said. "Look out, Al!" He reached over to snatch back the dreidel, but his hand knocked it off Little Al's fingertip. It took off flying across the room, hit the floor, and rolled out of sight under the sofa. Little Al scrambled after it.

Glaring at the boys, Mr. Hutchinson rose from his chair. But Isabel spoke before he could. "You people!" she cried, her voice teetering on the edge of tears.

"Isabel!" Mr. Levitsky said sharply.

"No, Papa!" she said. "They don't care about us! You said gentiles had no respect for us, and you were right!"

Isabel's father sprang from his chair, his hand up as if he were going to smack her. Isabel's eyes flashed fear, and she ran from the room.

✟ ❖ ✟

Chapter Ten

$\mathcal{M}$r. Levitsky muttered something in what Rudy assumed was Yiddish and sat down again. He shook his head at Jim Hutchinson and resumed their conversation. Mrs. Levitsky got up and stomped out behind Isabel.

"We was just kiddin' around," Little Al said out of the side of his mouth, for Rudy's ears alone. "I don't understand a doll like that."

"Yeah, me neither," Rudy said.

But he wasn't so sure about that. He wasn't sure exactly what he understood, but the whole scene had seemed familiar, and it bothered him. He was actually glad when Mrs. Levitsky returned with Isabel in tow, and Mr. Levitsky announced that it was time to open gifts. Isabel opened a package containing a pair of brown wool knee socks and said a stiff, "Thank you, Mama and Papa."

Little Al and Rudy each received dreidels of their own and were given another one to take home to Hildy Helen. When Mr. Levitsky put the last box into Dad's hands, he once again had tears in his eyes.

"Thank you for taking this to my Nathaniel," he said. "God bless you."

"We're going to the jail now?" Rudy said when they'd piled into a taxi again.

"Yes," Dad said. "And I don't want to hear any argument about it."

There was a tightness in Dad's voice.

"I'm disappointed in you two," Dad said.

"Why?" Rudy said. "We kept an eye on the girl."

"You made fun of her beliefs, right in her own home. I expected better."

That was all he said. Rudy didn't ask any more questions. He was sure that if he did, his father would bark, "The questions! Always the questions with you boys!"

Why did Mr. Levitsky keep saying that to us? Rudy thought. *And how come we get to ask anything we want, but Isabel isn't even allowed to talk?* His own thought surprised him. What did he care how Isabel Levitsky felt anyway?

Little Al evidently did care, because while they were waiting inside the jail for the guard to inspect Nathaniel's gift—"In case there's rod in there," Little Al explained to Rudy—Al asked, "Is that all that Isabel girl is gettin' for Christmas—well, Hanukkah—a pair of socks?"

"I doubt it," Dad said. "Jewish children open one present a night during Hanukkah."

Little Al's eyes lit up. "Eight presents! I wish I was Jewish!"

I don't! Rudy thought. *They can keep their dreidels and their menorahs and their latkes! I'm a Christian! God only loves Christians.*

When they were finally allowed to see Nathaniel, Little Al was full of things to tell him. He described the entire Hanukkah celebration as only Little Al could, while Nathaniel smiled mistily. Little Al finished up with a clap on Nathaniel's back, saying, "I never met any Jewish types before. You people sure know how to throw a party."

"You have, too, met Jewish people, Al," Dad said.

"Who?" Little Al said. "Who else do I know that's a Jew?"

"Maury and Dorothea Worthington," he said. "They're Jewish."

Rudy blinked. "They are?"

"Why would I make something like that up?" Dad said.

"I shoulda known," Rudy said, half to himself.

"Why is that?" Dad said.

"Because they're no good."

"Rudy!"

Dad's eyes cut into him, and Rudy couldn't return his angry stare. He looked away, just in time to see the sting on Nathaniel's face.

"Don't mind Rudy," Little Al said to him. "He's usually really a regular guy."

Nathaniel looked as if he wouldn't believe that if his life depended on it.

"Your family sends their love," Dad said, his voice still tight.

Nathaniel nodded. "How is my sister?"

"She's fine."

"I'd sure hate it if anything ever happened to her," Nathaniel said. "We're connected, us two. When she's scared, I feel it. When she cries, it goes right through my heart."

Rudy looked down at his galoshes. He didn't have to try to remember why that sounded familiar. He'd thought the same thing about his sister, just last night. For some reason, his cheeks began to burn. *Let's get out of here, Dad*, he thought.

When they did step out into the bitterly cold December night, Dad had just raised his hand to flag a taxi when a figure flung itself out of the shadows and into their path.

"Isabel?" Dad said. "You shouldn't be out in this weather."

"Papa sent me," she said. Under the ghostly lights of the police station, Rudy could see that there was frost stuck to her eyebrows, and her teeth were chattering. "They called just after you left, and then we tried calling the jail, but Papa was afraid you might not get the message, and—"

"Who called?"

"Your aunt or somebody! Something terrible has happened at your house, Mr. Hutchinson! You have to go home right away!"

All the way back to Prairie Avenue in the taxi, while Dad urged the driver to "step on it" every minute or so, Rudy felt his heart in his throat. When they squealed up in front of Aunt Gussie's and saw the ambulance, Dad threw a wad of money at the taxi driver and took the front lawn in three strides.

At the front door, a policeman stepped out and shone a torch into their faces. "Oh, it's you, Mr. Hutchinson," the officer said. "You'd better go in."

As if anyone could stop them. Rudy all but shoved past his father, his mind screaming, *Please, Jesus, don't let it be Hildy Helen. Not Hildy!*

They had to skid to a stop just inside the door. Two men with overcoats thrown over their white uniforms were leaning over someone who appeared to be lying on the front hall floor. Rudy did push past his father then, heart all the way in his throat, to see Sol being lifted onto a stretcher. His eyes were closed, his body was limp, and his face was as white as his hair, which stuck out from the edges of the bloody bandage wrapped around his head.

"Good heavens!" Dad said. "What happened?"

Neither Bridget nor Quintonia could answer. They stood huddled together, watching with eyes that bulged fear. And Aunt Gussie was otherwise occupied. At present, she had a man in a brown ulster coat and fedora backed up against the wall, her finger pointed directly at his nose.

"You'll find her, do you hear me?" she fairly screamed at him.

"If you need money to do it, I'll give you money. But you do whatever it takes to find her!"

Rudy took in the hall again. All the "hers" in the house were there—except one.

When she saw Rudy, Little Al, and Dad coming in, Aunt Gussie turned from the bug-eyed man long enough to say, "It's Hildy Helen! She's been taken!"

Before even he knew what he was doing, Rudy flew across the room and put his own face close to the man's.

"Where'd you take her? Where'd you take my sister? Bring her back, you hear me! You do what Aunt Gussie says! You get her back here!"

"Rudy, Rudy—"

His father curled his fingers around Rudy's arms and pulled him away. "Come on, son," he said.

His voice was trembling, too, but he firmly guided Rudy into the library. Brushing himself off, the man in the overcoat followed them.

"We were playing mah jongg here in the library," Aunt Gussie said when they were all seated. "Sol, Bridget, Hildy Helen, Quintonia, and myself. All of a sudden, it sounded as if my front door were being torn off the hinges."

"Looks like it, too," the man said. He opened his coat to pull out a pad and pencil, revealing a black shoulder holster and a shiny policeman's badge.

"Is that a plainclothes cop?" Rudy whispered to Little Al. Al nodded.

"Before any of us could even get up from this table," Aunt Gussie went on, "three men came barging in here."

"What did they look like?"

"Who could tell? They were all in big overcoats—all had hats pulled over their faces the way they do."

" 'They?' " the policeman said.

"It looked like the mob to me," Aunt Gussie said. "I'd have knocked one of their fool hats off if the lights hadn't gone out—and if my niece hadn't screamed."

"Hildy?" Rudy said. "What happened to her?"

Dad pressed his arm. "Go on, Auntie."

"Next thing I knew, there was a thud and more screaming. And then we heard the tires squealing away."

"What was the thud, do you think?"

"Sol hitting the floor," she said. "I felt him get up beside me, like he was going to go after them, the fool." She shook her head, and Rudy noticed for the first time that the skin around her mouth was almost blue. "They were brave, all of them," she said. "Bridget got to the lights and turned them on. And there was Quintonia, holding a vase up in the air like she was ready to hit someone. Unfortunately, the damage had already been done. Those hoodlums had already smashed something over Sol's head. We found him lying on the floor out there."

"And Hildy Helen?" Dad said.

Aunt Gussie closed her eyes. "She was nowhere to be found, James," she said. "While I was calling the police, Quintonia and Bridget looked everywhere. They took her. It's as plain as that." She pointed her eyes at the officer again. "And you, Detective Zorn, are wasting time standing here asking me the same questions over and over. Get out there and find that girl!"

She looked ready to push the poor man against the wall again, but she wobbled and fell back into the chair.

"Miss Gussie!" Quintonia cried. She took the room in a leap and pressed her fingers to Aunt Gussie's wrist.

"This woman is sick," she said, narrowing her eyes at Detective Zorn. "No more questions tonight. I'm puttin' her to bed."

Detective Zorn held up both hands in surrender.

Bridget poked her head in as Quintonia escorted Aunt Gussie

out. "I'll go to the hospital with Sol, Mr. Hutchinson," she said. "Call me if you hear anything about Hildy, would you?" She looked as shaken as the rest of them.

Dad could barely nod, and his neck was stiff with what Rudy knew was cold fear. He could feel his own teeth chattering, even when he gritted them together.

Detective Zorn sat down across from them and rested his folded hands on the table. They were shaking, too.

"We'll do everything we can to find your daughter and bring her home," he said. "But I'm going to need your help. Have you seen any suspicious characters around the neighborhood?"

Dad shook his head. "Beyond the phone call this afternoon, no."

Rudy sucked in his breath. Was it time to tell Dad about the man who had put a gun against his neck last night? *Was it only last night? It seems like a year ago! I shoulda told Dad before—and maybe this wouldn'ta happened.*

He leaned forward against the table. "Dad?" he said. "I saw some—"

Little Al tried to yank him back, but Rudy pulled himself away.

"What did you see?" Detective Zorn said, pencil poised over his pad.

Rudy blurted out the whole thing with Little Al breathing like a freight train behind him. *"Who cares about getting Maury Worthington now?"* Rudy wanted to shout at him. *"They've got Hildy!"*

When Rudy was finished, Detective Zorn scribbled a few more things onto his pad and stood up. "Like I said, we'll do all we can, Mr. Hutchinson," he said. "I'll call the minute we have anything."

Dad showed the detective to the front door, and Little Al got up and paced the room. From inside his cage, Picasso watched his every move, muttering nervously to himself. Even the bird was shaken into a frazzle.

"That's it?" Al said. "That's all they're going to do? You can't trust the coppers, is what I say."

"What else do you want them to do?" Rudy said.

"Why'd you have to tell 'em about last night?"

"Because! They had to know. Maybe it'll help 'em find Hildy."

"The way they're movin', they'll never find her—not without a lotta help."

"No, Al," Dad said from the doorway. "You are not going out there looking for Hildy Helen and that's final. Don't you try it, either one of you." His voice cracked. "I don't want another one of my children taken."

Little Al's face darkened into a scowl. Without a word, he marched from the room, and Rudy heard his galoshes stomping up the stairs. Rudy started to follow, but Dad took his arm.

"Rudy," he said. "I mean it. Please do as I say."

"Sure," Rudy said and shook his arm away. *If you hadn't taken this case for those Jews*, he thought as he headed for the stairs, *this never woulda happened, and you know it*.

He paused at the door to the room he shared with Little Al, but he didn't go in. The only person he wanted to talk to right now was Hildy Helen.

His throat grew tight, and he went down the hall to her room. Her bed was rumpled from her climbing out of it to go downstairs to play a game. He threw himself onto it, and he could smell the last traces of witch hazel.

I wish it was last night again and she was lying right here, he thought, his throat squeezing in as if it were in a vice. *Last night all she cared about was not getting to do her whole dance—about somebody messing up her performance*.

Rudy rolled over and looked up at the ceiling. *Jesus, take me back*, he prayed. *Make it so that's the worst thing she has to worry about*.

He closed his eyes and kept telling himself over and over that it would come true because he was a Christian. But as he drifted off to sleep, he wasn't so sure he believed that anymore.

He was dreaming of Hildy Helen, dancing like a snowflake outside, slipping on the ice, and being picked up by a man in a fedora who climbed out of a car, when his eyes suddenly sprang open.

"Rudy," his father was saying in a voice purple with rage, "Rudy, where is Little Al?"

Rudy sat up, heart pounding. "He didn't come in here with me. He's in our room," he said.

"No, he isn't," Dad said. "Little Al is gone."

✝ ✦ ✝

Chapter Eleven

*F*or the rest of the night, Rudy and his father sat in the library, waiting for a phone call, waiting for the delivery of a ransom note, and waiting for the sun to come up.

When it finally did, Rudy had just fallen asleep with his head on the table. Dad opened the drapes and stood looking out at the gray morning as Rudy blinked himself awake.

"What is it going to take, Rudy?" Dad said.

Rudy blinked again.

"What do I have to do to convince that boy that he can't take on the mob like it's some street gang?"

Rudy shrugged. He was pretty angry with Little Al himself. Wasn't it bad enough that Hildy Helen was missing? He pulled his legs up into the chair and hugged them to his chest. This was the most alone he'd felt in a long time.

This must be what Nathaniel feels like in that jail, he thought.

He was stunned by the thought.

Dad went to the desk and sank into Aunt Gussie's chair. He rubbed his hand across his face. A couple of times he looked like he was about to say something, but nothing came out.

Rudy felt his throat go tight again. Was Dad giving up? If he was, there really wouldn't be any hope.

"Go get dressed, Rudy," he said suddenly. "You and I are going out. I can't just sit around here waiting."

When Rudy came down in his coat and muffler, Dad had Sol's car keys in his hand. Quintonia was standing next to him, looking baggy-eyed and weary.

"I'll call Dr. Kennedy, Mr. Jim," she said. "I think it's more than the shock that got to her."

"You haven't told her about Alonzo?"

"No, sir, and I ain't goin' to, if it's all the same to you."

Dad nodded grimly. "I'll stay in touch wherever we are."

They went first to the hospital on Polk Street, where Bridget had spent the night at Sol's bedside. The old chauffeur was propped up in bed, but his eyes seemed unfocused, and Rudy wasn't sure he recognized them at all, though he did follow Bridget with his gaze whenever she moved around the room.

"He doesn't seem to remember anything," Bridget whispered to them. "The doctor says his memory may come back, but it's too soon to tell."

In quick but quiet tones Dad brought Bridget up to date on Hildy and Little Al. All Bridget could do was shake her head. With a sigh Dad touched Sol's sagging shoulder and turned to go, beckoning Rudy to follow.

Dad was silent all the way to the South State Street police station, where Detective Zorn had his office. Even there, he asked the officer clipped questions, nodded without a word, and led Rudy out. His face was pinched so tightly, Rudy didn't dare ask where they were going next.

He was surprised, however, when they turned onto Douglas Boulevard in Lawndale and parked in front of the Levitsky's grocery. Protesting was, of course, out of the question.

Inside, Uriah was reading in a chair next to the furnace. Mrs. Levitsky hurried into the back at the snap of his fingers, and she and Isabel emerged with the inevitable pickled herring. Rudy didn't care how rude it was, he knew he would never get a mouthful of it down today. He was surprised when Isabel stood next to him and said in a low voice, "Do you want to come in the kitchen? It's boring out here."

When they got to the back room, she nodded him to a stool and uncovered a plate of leftover *rugalach*. Rudy watched her carefully as he took a piece.

"You didn't poison these, did you?" he said.

Her little eyes poked out like pencil points.

"I'm just razzin' ya," Rudy said. "My dad says I shouldn'ta made fun of your dreidel last night."

She poked her finger into the raisin filling. "I heard about your sister and brother. I know how I felt when they took *my* brother away."

"Oh," Rudy said.

" 'Course, it's different for you, being a boy. They probably listen to you."

"I guess," Rudy said.

"You're lucky," she said. "Nobody ever listens to me, especially when there's trouble. Except Nathaniel."

She chewed at her thick bottom lip and was quiet for a minute. Rudy nibbled at the *rugalach*, but suddenly it was as tasteless as an eraser.

"I hear and see a lot of things adults don't," Isabel said. "But they never believe me." She looked at him sideways. "You should keep your eyes open. Being a boy and all, your father might believe you if you find out anything."

"They don't ever listen to you, not ever?" Rudy said.

Isabel shrugged. "I'll pray for your sister and brother," she said.

It was Rudy's turn to bite his lip. Somehow it didn't seem

right to say, "But what good would that do? God won't listen to you. You're Jewish."

Besides, he didn't want her to run out and leave him here. At least when she was talking, he didn't feel quite so alone.

His father didn't stay long talking to Uriah Levitsky, and it was still light when they got back into the Pierce Arrow and headed for Prairie Avenue.

"I've called Quintonia three times," Dad said. "Still no word on either of them. Quintonia says Dr. Kennedy wants to do some tests on Aunt Gussie."

Rudy looked out the window. He never got to sit in the front seat, and yet there was no thrill in it now. Nor did the Christmas garlands or the wreaths hanging on shop doors mean anything. It wasn't Christmas without Hildy Helen and Little Al. And it wasn't without Aunt Gussie, either.

Suddenly it hurt even to think. He was about to turn away from the window when he caught sight of something that made his heart skip.

"Dad, stop!" he said.

Dad's foot at once went to the brake.

"What is it?"

"Right there—at the stoplight—right in front. Do you see that car?"

Dad followed Rudy's pointing finger to the long black car on the other side of the intersection. "The Packard?"

"Yeah, that's the car I saw last night—the one that man got out of."

"The one who came after you?"

"That's it! I know it is!"

Dad didn't even hesitate. When the light turned green, he turned sharply down the side street and sped around the block. They pulled out just two cars behind the Packard.

"Keep him in your sights, Rudy," Dad said. "I have to be careful on this ice, but we don't want to lose them."

Rudy rode with his face pressed to the window, his heart pounding its way up his chest as he called out directions.

"They're turning onto Michigan Avenue. They're slowing down. He's going down 22nd, Dad. Don't slow down or you'll lose him!"

"You know your onions, Rudy," Dad said. "Those are the bad guys, all right." He pulled the Pierce Arrow into the stockyard of a smoke-stained factory and turned off the motor. "And I know where they went."

"Where?"

"Just as I thought—the Lexington Hotel."

"How'd you know that?"

Dad opened the car door. "That's where Al Capone has his office."

Dad pulled his fedora low on his face and stuffed his hands into his pockets. With his cheeks pinched in, Rudy thought he could have passed for a mobster, at least from a hundred paces away. He had to almost run to keep up with him.

"That's the Lexington?" Rudy said, pointing to a posh-looking structure with a red, velvety awning stretching over its entryway.

"Pretty ritzy, eh?" Dad said.

If Rudy hadn't known his father better, he'd have sworn that was hate he heard edging Dad's voice.

"It's a grand place," Dad went on as they walked, frosty air puffing thickly from their mouths and noses. "They say he has 10 rooms there, although he personally only uses one on the corner of the top floor. When he's there, he sits in a chair with a bullet-proof back, and he has to take the freight elevator up and down with a crew of bodyguards. He thinks he's powerful, but he sounds like a prisoner to me."

"So's Hildy Helen," Rudy said.

Dad didn't answer, but his face tightened even more. "Rumor

has it he brought a whole slew of laborers from Italy to build a network of tunnels from the hotel to other buildings. And that's not the only network he has." Dad grunted. "They say his desk is covered with phones that connect him with politicians, judges, and police officials."

"Police!" Rudy said. His heart was back in his throat again. "You don't think they're on Al Capone's side do you? You don't think they know where Hildy Helen is and they're not telling us?"

"I'm trying not to think that," Dad said. "But I'm afraid that's what Little Al was thinking when he took off."

Dad suddenly pressed his hand into Rudy's shoulder and they stopped, down one block and across the street from the Lexington. "All right, there are the men from the car—see, standing in the doorway?"

"Is the doorman a mobster, too?" Rudy said.

"There's no telling who's on the mobsters' payroll," Dad said. "But right now, I don't think we have any choice but to count on one policeman I think I can trust." He leaned down to put his face close to Rudy's. "I want you to get to the State Street station, son," he said. "Take the back alleys, do whatever you have to, but get there and tell Detective Zorn where I am. Then you wait for me there until I come back to get you."

"What are you gonna do?" Rudy said.

"I'm going to stay put and keep my eye on these two. Tell Zorn that if our car is gone, he'll know I've followed them."

Rudy nodded and backed away. Dad set his eyes on the hotel and didn't look up as Rudy finally turned and ran off down 23rd Street. Rudy didn't look back after that. It took all his concentration to zigzag his way off the main streets, down the icy alleys and side roads—something Little Al could have done with ease.

Why aren't you here with me now? Rudy thought angrily. *Why'd you have to go and run off? I need you!*

Darkness was already falling, and Rudy had a hard time spotting the icy places. Twice he fell and then had to run in soaked knickers. By the time the eerie blue-lit sign at the police station came into view, he couldn't feel anything but his chest, where his heart was banging like a trip-hammer.

His hands were so frozen he could barely get the front door open. When he did, he ran straight into a young man wearing an open overcoat and the telltale press pass in his hatband. He shoved Rudy out of the way and burst out the door. Rudy stumbled inside, only to collide with still another reporter. This one was older, and he was obviously angry.

"Lieutenant!" the older reporter called out. "What do you people mean pushing my people around?"

"Whatsa matter, Sam?" said the officer behind the front desk. He had the staccato voice all policemen in Chicago seemed to have.

"We go up to the news bureau upstairs, just like we always do," Sam said. "And a coupla your plainclothes men frisked us! They have one heck of a nerve if you ask me!"

The lieutenant shifted his eyes. "Those aren't my men."

"Then who in the Sam Hill are they?"

"Those are Capone's men."

"Says you!"

Rudy didn't wait to hear the rest. He wasn't sure he could have if he'd stayed. His heart was drumming in his ears.

But before he could get back out the front door, he felt a hand on the back of his collar, and he froze. Every story Little Al had ever told him about Al Capone raced through his head.

"You're young Hutchinson, aren't you?" a slightly familiar voice said.

Rudy twisted to look up. It was Detective Zorn. He didn't know whether to be relieved or not.

"What are you doing here, son?" Zorn said. "I thought your father was going to keep you under wraps."

Dad had told him to tell Detective Zorn. He couldn't though, not if the police station was under Capone's control. Even Officer O'Dell had said—

But what if he didn't tell? What might happen?

Please, Jesus, he prayed. *Tell me whether I should trust this fella!*

There was no answer. There wasn't even a picture in his head.

"Son?" Detective Zorn said. "What's going on?"

Rudy closed his eyes, drew a deep breath and spilled out the story. Detective Zorn let go of Rudy's collar and patted his shoulder.

"I'll go right over to the Lexington," he said.

Rudy started to follow him out, but he put up his hand. Even though Rudy hadn't told him what Dad had said about waiting at the police station, Detective Zorn said, "I think you'd better stay here." Then he turned to the officer behind the desk and said, "Lieutenant, take care of our friend here, would you?"

"No!" Rudy said.

But Detective Zorn was already gone, and the lieutenant was out from behind the counter. He was tall and broad-shouldered and his arms were long enough that he could have caught Rudy even if he'd been twice as far away. Rudy sagged.

If these fellas really are taking orders from Capone, I might have just set a trap for Dad, he thought.

"Don't worry, we'll take good care of ya," the lieutenant said. "Why don't I get you something to eat. And then you can go in and see your friend."

"My friend?"

"Hey, Joe!" the lieutenant called out. "Bring the Jew-boy out, would ya? Put him in the visitor's room."

Rudy felt himself cringe.

"I tell you one thing I've learned from that kid," the lieutenant said as he led Rudy off down a narrow, gray-walled hall.

"Them Jews can't play cards worth a hoot."

The lieutenant provided Rudy with a cheese sandwich and a small bottle of milk. It all went down like cardboard as the officer went on about how kids these days couldn't seem to stay out of trouble and how he hoped Rudy would learn from his friend's mistake.

"I don't mind him bein' a Jew-boy," he said. "But a Jew-boy shootin' people—unh-uh, that don't fly with me."

Rudy dropped the uneaten half of his sandwich onto the plate and wiped his hands on his wet knickers. "I'd like to see him now," he said. Right now anybody else would be a better person to talk to than this lieutenant.

The officer shrugged and let him into the room where he and Dad and Little Al had met with Nathaniel the night before. The day before that, Hildy Helen had been with them in that room. It made Rudy's throat tighten, as if the sandwich were stuck there.

"Hello," Nathaniel said to him. His voice was cool, and his handsome face was steely-still.

"Hello," Rudy said. He looked down at the table and felt himself going crimson. Until just this minute, he'd forgotten the last thing he'd said in this room: "They're no good." He'd been talking about Maury and Dorothea, but both he and Nathaniel knew all Jewish people were included. And it was obvious Nathaniel hadn't forgotten it.

"Your sister's fine," Rudy blurted out. "I talked to her just a little while ago."

"Thanks," Nathaniel said coldly. "I hope you weren't as rude to her as you were to me."

"Not today," Rudy said. "I was last night, but I was pretty nice today."

"At least you're honest," Nathaniel said. "Will you tell me the truth if I ask you what you're doing here?"

"Sure," Rudy said. He fiddled with his fingers. Nathaniel's direct manner made him as nervous as Aunt Gussie did when she caught him using one of her artifacts as a slingshot or something. His mind started to drift to what was going to happen to Aunt Gussie now.

Nathaniel interrupted his thoughts. "So, what are you doing here? Does your father think maybe I'll tell you something I wouldn't tell him?"

"No!" Rudy said. "Besides, you can tell my dad anything. He's even more honest than me."

There was a silence. Nathaniel seemed to have no desire to strike up a conversation.

"I'm in here because I couldn't stand talking to that lieutenant fella any longer," Rudy said.

Nathaniel sniffed. "I'm glad to know I'm at least better than he is in your estimation."

Rudy didn't know what estimation meant, but it was pretty clear that Nathaniel was a smart kid.

"Where do you go to school?" he said.

"The *beth hamedrash*," Nathaniel said.

"Who is she, anyway?" Rudy said. "I saw her name all over Lawndale."

Nathaniel smiled faintly. "You don't get out much, do you, kid? Every temple has a *beth hamedrash*. It's where we go to study the Torah and the Talmud. The Torah is what you call the Old Testament."

"You study the Bible?" Rudy said. "How come? That's a Christian book!"

"Where do you think you people got it?" Nathaniel said. "At least the Old Testament. All those old fellas, Moses and Abraham, they were all Jews. Jesus was a Jew."

Rudy jerked up in his chair. "Says you!"

"Read it for yourself, if you don't believe me," Nathaniel said.

"It's right there in your New Testament."

Rudy rolled his eyes. This kid was obviously not as smart as he'd thought.

They lapsed into another silence. Finally, Nathaniel said, "So tell me about Isabel, if you can do it without insulting her."

"There's not much to tell. We mostly just talked about my sister getting kidnapped and my brother running off to go find her."

Nathaniel's eyes sprang open. "You're not giving me the business?"

"Huh," Rudy said. "I wouldn't fool about them."

"At least you have *some* integrity," Nathaniel said.

Rudy didn't know what that was, either, but he sure wasn't going to ask this fella. He wriggled in the chair. "At least my father listens to me, just like Isabel said he would. She says nobody listens to her."

"Except me," Nathaniel said. His face lost its hard shine. He looked suddenly sad.

"How come nobody else listens to her?" Rudy said. "She says she's seen and heard things adults don't hear and see, only nobody'll pay any attention to what she has to say. I saw your father doing it. Last night he wouldn't even let her talk."

Nathaniel leaned so abruptly across the table, Rudy was startled.

"She said that? She said she's heard things? Seen things she hasn't told anybody?"

"Yeah," Rudy said. "She hasn't told anybody because nobody'll listen."

"I'd listen," Nathaniel said. He got up and paced restlessly around the room, his hands fastened in front of him with the handcuffs. Rudy's eyes stuck to them.

"She knows something. I know she does," Nathaniel said. "I wish they'd let her come see me."

"Fat chance," Rudy said. "Your father won't even let her answer a question. I don't think he's gonna let her come see you."

"You're right about that," Nathaniel said, nodding. His eyes suddenly darted to Rudy, and he came back to the table. "You have to get it out of her, Hutchinson."

"Me?" Rudy said. "How am I gonna do that?"

"Get her to trust you, the way she does me. She'd tell me anything. If she knew you'd listen to her and that you'd tell only me what you heard from her, she'd tell you about anything."

"I don't know if I can do that."

"I doubt you can either," Nathaniel said. "But you have to try."

Rudy bristled. "Why?"

"Because, if somebody could get information about your brother and sister, you'd want them to do it. You can at least give me that, can't you?"

"He's right in here," said a voice from the doorway.

The lieutenant let Jim Hutchinson in and closed the door behind him. Rudy felt himself melting in relief. But he also knew from his father's face that he hadn't gotten anything from the mobsters in the Packard.

"The police questioned them," Dad said woodenly. "But they said there wasn't any evidence to arrest them—or anything that would lead us to Hildy Helen." He sighed. "Detective Zorn has promised to keep an eye on them."

Rudy grunted. Little Al was probably doing that much—and at least they could trust him. Something clutched at his chest, and he put his hand up to it. It didn't take much to realize it was just plain fear. He looked at Nathaniel. The Jewish boy was boring his eyes right into him.

"My sister knows just how you feel," Nathaniel said softly.

Dad assured Nathaniel that as soon as Hildy Helen and Little Al were found, he would be back to work on his case. "I have some people looking into some things in the meantime," he said. "Try to keep your chin up."

Nathaniel nodded as the lieutenant came in to lead him back to his cell. Rudy watched them go down the hall.

"You coming, Rudy?" Dad said.

"Yeah," Rudy said. Then he raised his voice. "Dad, can I go see Isabel tomorrow?"

He glanced over his shoulder. Nathaniel was looking back. Once again, he gave a quiet nod.

✢ ⚜ ✢

Chapter Twelve

*A*s Dad drove him toward Lawndale the next day, Rudy spotted wreath after wreath on door after door. *Oh, yeah,
Christmas is coming,* he thought. At the moment he didn't feel
like counting the days. The wreaths were starting to remind him
more of a funeral than a holiday.

"Call when you're ready to come home," Dad said when he
left Rudy at the Levitskys'.

Rudy was ready within about two minutes. Isabel set a plate
of *sufganiyot* in front of him and sat on the other side of the table
blinking at him while he ate. Every attempt to get her to talk was
met with either a nod or a shrug.

*I guess she said everything she ever wanted to say to me yes-
terday*, he thought. He wasn't used to a sister who didn't talk.
The thought of Hildy Helen went through him like a blade.

Well, if she wasn't going to talk, maybe he should. She was
bound to blurt something out sooner or later.

Of course, what there was to talk about Rudy hadn't a clue.
Jesus, help me, he prayed.

Again, there was no answer, no drawing in his head. He just
had to plunge right in.

"You know what Nathaniel tried to tell me last night?" he said.

"What?" Isabel said.

"He said Jesus was a Jew!"

Isabel shrugged.

"You have to admit that's pretty crazy," Rudy said. "Jesus was a Christian!"

Isabel slid out of her chair and went to the curtain that separated the back room from the store and peeked out as if checking to see if the coast was clear. When she turned back to Rudy, she spoke in a low voice. "Jesus couldn't have been a Christian," she said. "There was no such thing as a Christian back then. Jesus was a Jew. Nathaniel showed it to me in the Bible."

"If it's true," Rudy said, "how come you're whispering?"

"Because," she said, "Papa doesn't know Nathaniel has read the New Testament. And he doesn't know Nathaniel teaches me the things he learns at *beth hamedrash.*"

"Why would he care about that?" Rudy said. "My dad wants me and Hildy Helen to learn everything in the world. It even gets to be a pain sometimes."

Isabel blinked. "I'm a girl," she said simply.

"So?"

"It isn't important for a Jewish girl to be educated. She just needs to find a husband and get married."

Good luck, Rudy thought automatically. But he grinned at her. "You're lucky they don't make you learn a bunch of stuff and ask you a bunch of questions. You oughta hear my Aunt Gussie after we've been to church. She gives us a test at the dinner table every Sunday afternoon—what the sermon was about, what the gospel lesson was about. It's worse than school."

"Oh," Isabel said. Her face was wistful, and Rudy felt a pang of guilt.

"I'm sorry I made fun of your dreidel the other night," he said suddenly.

Once again she shrugged, and silence fell. When the curtain

opened, Rudy was glad even though it was Uriah Levitsky who stood in the doorway. He was beginning to dislike the man.

"Isabel," Mr. Levitsky said in the sharp voice he seemed to reserve only for her, "make a delivery for me. You can take your friend with you. You need someone with sense along with you."

I'm not supposed to go out without an adult, Rudy thought. But Uriah disappeared behind the curtain again and Isabel followed to get her instructions.

"Wait right here," she said to Rudy. There was a hint of a smile in her eyes. Rudy decided maybe it didn't count, going out on this side of town.

Nobody knows me over here, he decided. *Even Dad said it was safer here than on Prairie. Officer O'Dell said it, too.*

He pushed thoughts of Hildy Helen out of his head and put on his coat.

The air was so cold and dry as they headed up Douglas Boulevard, it made Rudy gasp. They walked at an almost-run, their galoshes squeaking on the tightly packed snow. You didn't linger on a day like this. Even the pigeons huddled in the eaves to escape the wintry blast, and the sun itself was a mere dying gleam in the pale December sky.

They walked longer than Rudy had expected to, away from the squiggly-writing signs of Lawndale and into downtown. Isabel delivered her father's package to a rich-looking shop where an elegant menorah stood in the window. Rudy was grateful to stand inside the entryway and warm his toes near the radiator. The shopkeeper, however, didn't seem grateful to have him there. He gave Rudy a sour look.

"What did I ever do to him?" Rudy said to Isabel as they hurried out of the shop, back out into the cold.

"He doesn't like gentiles," Isabel said.

"That's pretty lousy!" Rudy said. "He doesn't even know me!"

Isabel looked at him and blinked again. This time, there was nothing blank about her eyes.

"What do you suppose is going on over there?" they overheard a passer-by say.

Rudy looked where the man was staring. Across the street by the river, a small crowd had gathered, and all were pointing and gesturing excitedly.

"Let's go have a look," Rudy said to Isabel. That was what Little Al would have done.

They dodged the traffic going across the street and joined the crowd, who were all looking down into the icy-gray Chicago River. There were two policemen down there, and they were dragging something from the water.

"My stars, it's a body!" someone cried.

Rudy craned to see, but a pair of gloved hands went down over his eyes.

"Don't look, boy," said a woman. "You're too young for this."

Rudy twisted away from her hand in time to see a large chunk of ice with something in it being hauled up the bank.

"That's a body?" Rudy said.

"Looks like a young man," the woman said. "I tell you, boy, take your friend and go on home. You don't need to see this."

But Rudy's heart had already pounded its way into his throat, and he pushed viciously past her to get to the edge. Could it be Little Al? *Please, Jesus, don't let it be Little Al! Please!*

Then Isabel screamed. She was hollering something in Yiddish, her hands clamped to the sides of her face, and for a confused moment he thought it must be Nathaniel encased in that ice cube.

"That boy's been dead for days," one man said.

"Look, he was shot, too!" someone else pointed out.

Isabel took one more look at the stiff and frozen body and then turned and broke out of the crowd. Rudy took off after her.

"Did you know that boy?" he said when he caught up to her.

"Did I know him? Such a question!" she said. Her voice was crackly and high-pitched, the way her father's got when he was worked up. "Of course I know him."

"Who is he—was he?"

"He was a friend of Nathaniel's. He was in the Miller gang with him." Isabel's face crumpled. "He used to bring me licorice when he came for Nathaniel. I really love licorice."

She cried all the way back to Lawndale. Rudy walked beside her with his hands stuffed into the pockets of his coat. He didn't know what to say.

He did know one thing, though, and he couldn't shake it when he arrived back at the grocery. He called his father and waited in the store for him to come for him.

Another member of the Miller gang had been destroyed. First Nathaniel by being thrown into jail. Now this one, first shot, then tossed into an ice-water grave.

Didn't that make it look like Nathaniel hadn't shot Victor Vedoli? Wasn't it pretty clear that somebody was out to get the Miller gang?

As he watched the Pierce Arrow pull up, Rudy shuddered. Whoever it was, they didn't play around when they were "getting" someone. What if they were the same people who were out to "get" Dad by taking Hildy Helen? What might they do to her?

He told Dad the story on the way home, and his father's face grew even more grim than it had been ever since last night. When they got home, he went straight into the library and closed the door. Rudy could hear him using the telephone.

Aunt Gussie was still in bed, and Quintonia was in there tending to her. Bridget was still at the hospital with Sol. Even Picasso kept to the back of his cage, one wing over his face.

Rudy wandered aimlessly into his empty room and flopped down on the bed. The wet galoshes came off, but he kept his coat and muffler on. It had been so cold outside, he didn't think he'd ever be warm again, inside or out. He was discovering that loneliness was a very chilly feeling.

I'm so mad at you, Little Al! he thought up at the ceiling. *You could help me figure this all out. Isabel liked you. She would already have told you everything. Together, we could probably find Hildy Helen, too—before those gangsters do something terrible to her.*

He rolled over, away from his thoughts. Something felt lumpy underneath him, and he pulled it out.

It was Little Al's Windsor cap, and his muffler, too, and his mackinaw coat. He never hung anything up.

Rudy sat straight up on the bed. Little Al never went out without his coat and hat. Besides, why would he go off looking for Hildy Helen in his shirtsleeves in weather like this?

The image of the dead body being hauled up the river bank in a block of ice made him shiver.

"Little Al wouldn't have left here without his coat!" he said out loud. "If he did, he's frozen to death by now!"

Rudy gave his head a hard shake. No, that wasn't it. That couldn't be it. Little Al hadn't left there on his own. Otherwise he would have let Rudy know where he was by now. He always did. Rudy had been so busy being angry, he hadn't stopped to think how Little Al was—that he would never let Rudy worry like this if he could help it. He'd promised to always protect Rudy.

Rudy jumped off the bed and took the steps downstairs two at a time. His father had to know about this.

But Dad wasn't in the library. There was only a note saying he'd gone to the office. Rudy went straight to the phone, but the receiver was dead, and one look out the window explained why. The snow was coming down again, probably bogging down the phone line somewhere.

Rudy replaced the phone to its candlestick and tried to think.

Dad said don't go out without someone, but there is no one!

The loneliness descended, heavier and colder than the snow, and Rudy tried to shake it off as if he were dusting off snowflakes. Then he went for his mackinaw coat and muffler. The police might not have any evidence against Al Capone's men, but that was only because they didn't see and hear the things kids could.

Sorry, Dad, he thought, and he slipped out the front door into the frigid night.

It was almost dark by the time he got to the Lexington Hotel. The lobby windows were cheerily lit with Christmas lights and hung with wreaths.

How dare you celebrate Christmas? Rudy thought angrily. *You're no more Christians than the Levitskys are!*

"Rudy—is that you?"

Rudy nearly jumped out of his skin. It was Isabel Levitsky. For a shocked moment, he was certain she'd heard his thoughts.

But if she had, she wasn't thinking about that. She blew into her hands to warm her face and stomped her feet on the sidewalk.

"What are you doing here?" he said.

"I followed you," she said.

"From where?"

"Your house."

Rudy stared. "Why?"

"Because I wanted to tell you something." She crossed her arms over her chest and stuck her hands in her armpits. Rudy did the same. It was warmer that way.

"What did you want to tell me?" he said.

"Those Italians didn't accidentally shoot that Victor boy. They planned on it all along."

"How do you know?"

"One day before the shooting, I was delivering something on the West Side for Papa, and I saw them on the corner. I don't like to walk past them. They always spit at me."

"They spit at you?"

"So I went down an alley, and I could hear them talking plain as day from there. I heard them say 'Miller gang,' so I stopped and listened."

Rudy knew that at this point, Little Al would have said, "I like a doll like you!"

"They said Victor was really trying to be a big shot with 'the Boss.' They said he knew he was going to get shot in the leg and he wanted it. They said he'd do anything to get the Boss's attention."

"Somebody would do that?"

"They said he would. I don't know why. I've seen the Boss's men come in Papa's grocery. They're ugly and evil. I wouldn't do anything for them!"

Perhaps if it had been another time, another situation, Rudy would have laughed. Isabel's face was fierce, and she stomped her foot just the way Hildy Helen did when she didn't get her own way. Now he could see why Nathaniel cared so much about his sister.

"Why didn't you tell your father?" Rudy said.

She didn't have to answer. Nobody ever listened to Isabel.

"I think we should go to my dad's office," he said. "You can tell him what you just told me."

Isabel took a step backward.

"All right," Rudy said. "I'll tell him for you, but you have to come with me. He'll believe you—even if you are a girl."

Isabel nodded slowly.

They both pulled up the lapels of their coats and started into the wind that blew across Michigan Avenue, but Rudy stopped. Two men came out the front door of the Lexington. Rudy could make out only their silhouettes, but their outlines were unmistakable. One had a head shaped like a bullet. They strode quickly toward the long black Packard parked a block away.

"Wait," Rudy whispered. "First we have to follow those men. They might take us to Hildy Helen and maybe even Little Al. I know you want to help your brother, but—"

"—you want to help yours, too," Isabel said. She tugged at Rudy's coat sleeve. "Are they going somewhere in a car?"

"That Packard down there."

"How are we going to keep up with them on foot?"

Rudy groaned. The two men stopped and turned, as if they'd heard him. Rudy grabbed the back of Isabel's coat and pulled her behind a sign he knew barely covered one of them, much less two. But the men headed for the door of the hotel again, waving their arms at each other as if they were arguing.

"They must have forgotten something," Rudy said.

"Come on," Isabel whispered.

"Where are we going?"

"We're getting in the car."

"Are you nuts? They'll see us!"

"Not in the back, and not when it's this dark. Now, come on!"

"Say, you're pretty good at this," Rudy said as they took off at a run across the street.

"How do you think I find out things adults never see or hear?" she said.

They'd barely climbed into the back seat of the Packard when they heard the loud, argumentative voices of the two men coming down the sidewalk again.

"Adults argue a lot," Isabel whispered to Rudy. "That's why they don't hear things. They're too busy talking all the time."

Rudy looked closely at Isabel. She sure didn't look as scared as he felt. Her small eyes were alert and bright, and those thick lips were almost smiling. He decided she was nearly as spunky as Little Al. That made him feel better as the doors opened, the two thugs climbed in, and the Packard took off down Michigan Avenue.

The storm had kicked up so hard by now, they could feel the heavy car swaying in the frigid wind blowing off Lake Michigan.

"I can't depend on you. I told the Boss. I can't depend on you," one of the men said.

"You can't depend on me? Whatta ya talkin'? It's you forgot the bags of stuff, not me."

"I tol' you to get 'em."

"And I said get 'em yerself."

Rudy looked at Isabel. She was rolling her eyes and shaking her head.

The men continued to snap at each other until the Packard finally pulled to a stop. "This is one miserable place," the driver said.

"You said it," his passenger muttered.

It was the first thing they'd agreed on since they'd left the Lexington.

The doors opened and closed, and the men's shoes crunched across the snow. When their footsteps finally faded and a building door slammed, Isabel poked Rudy and they both rose slowly until they could look out the back window. It was so frosty, though, all they could see were snowy crystals.

"Do we get out and look?" Rudy said.

Isabel nodded and pushed open the door. The cold air hit them like a wall of ice. Rudy's lips stiffened before he'd gone three steps, and he wondered how he had ever thought that some people just made a big deal out of the cold. The famous wind in this city seemed to cut holes in the warmest coat.

"Look," Isabel whispered into the side of his cap, "there's a fire escape. We can look down through that window."

"But they're on the first floor," Rudy whispered back.

"It's a warehouse," Isabel said. "There's only one floor."

"Oh," Rudy said.

He followed her across the yard—it looked like a deserted railroad yard—and climbed up the fire escape behind her. For a girl so thick, she wasn't clumsy. She wasn't the one whose foot slipped on an icy metal step. She *was* the one who reached back a hand to steady Rudy.

But there was no time to feel embarrassed. The minute Rudy got to the fire escape landing and brushed the snow off the window, he forgot himself.

There on the ground inside the warehouse, far below them, lay Hildy Helen, tied with a rope, a gag over her mouth.

And next to her lay Little Al.

✝ ✝ ✝

Chapter Thirteen

*R*udy let out a cry, which was muffled at once by Isabel's hand over his mouth.

"Shhh!" she hissed at him.

Rudy nodded, but he had to keep his own hand across his lips for fear he'd yell their names.

"Are they alive?" he whispered through his mittened fingers.

Isabel didn't dare answer, for just then the two men came into view, each one carrying a bulging paper sack. The first, the one with the bullet-shaped head, stuck out the toe of his pointed button shoes and poked Al in the side. The little Italian's eyes sprang open, and even from high on the fire escape, Rudy could see the glint of anger in them. Little Al was definitely alive.

So was Hildy Helen. The other man was shorter in stature and had evidently taken great care dressing up. His pressed trousers had a razor-sharp crease and his camel overcoat had a high waistband and lapels that stuck up over his shoulders. He squatted down next to Hildy. She wriggled away and gave him a look that should have frozen him solid on the spot.

The men started to talk, and Isabel pressed her ear to the glass. Rudy wanted to listen too, but the landing was too narrow and the window too small for both of them to eavesdrop.

"What are they saying?" Rudy said.

"Shhh!"

Rudy waited. His stomach felt like the mainspring of a clock, winding tighter and tighter with each second.

Finally Isabel whispered again. "They said they're going to take their gags off and feed them. But the brats better keep their yaps shut or they'll be sorry."

"The hoods are the ones who are gonna be sorry!" Rudy couldn't imagine Hildy Helen or Little Al keeping their mouths shut under most circumstances. This situation practically begged for a mouthful from both of them.

But when the men yanked the gags out of the children's mouths and proceeded to pull loaves of bread and hunks of salami out of the sacks, neither Hildy Helen nor Little Al spoke a word.

"What did they do to them?" Rudy said.

"Would you shush? I can't hear!"

Isabel once again had her ear pressed to the glass. Rudy put his hand back over his mouth and watched. Little Al was eating the bread like there was no tomorrow. Hildy Helen nibbled at the crust on her bread and turned her head.

"She has to have butter on her bread," Rudy whispered.

"The tall one wants a cuppa joe," Isabel said, still listening and nodding at the window. "The spiffy dresser says no, he's too clumsy and is sure to spill it." Isabel rolled her eyes. "I bet he shops at that place on Halsted Street—Men's Snappy Furnishings Store."

"What's he saying to Hildy Helen?"

"He's saying, 'Eat this, ya little brat! We paid five cents a loaf for this bread!' "

"She's not a brat!"

"He thinks she is." Isabel listened again. "I think the other guy's reciting poetry."

"Says you!"

"He said, 'Past the lips and over the tongue, look out stomach, here I come.' "

Evidently Little Al didn't appreciate the fine art of verse, because just then he spit out an entire mouthful of bread and salami, which landed in the middle of the man's chest and dribbled slowly down.

Isabel gave Rudy a solemn look. "I'm not gonna repeat what he's saying now," she said.

Rudy nodded and watched through the window.

The men were stuffing the gags back into Little Al's and Hildy Helen's mouths. Then they tossed the remains of the measly supper back into the sacks, and Bullet Head heaved both bags into a corner.

Spiffy Dresser took off his derby, smoothed a hand over his hair that shone like patent leather, and carefully replaced the hat.

"Hey," Rudy whispered, "it looks like they're leaving!"

"Get low!" Isabel said.

They both hunkered down on the step and tried to flatten themselves against the brick wall, which was hard for Isabel to do with her chunky form.

We might as well just stand up and say, "Here! We're up here!" Rudy thought. His heart pounded.

Below, the door opened and slammed shut, and voices rose right to them.

"I hope the Boss starts baiting their old man soon," one of them said. "I'm getting sick of this."

"You said it. I ain't no baby-sitter," said the other one.

"You ain't no baby-sitter? What about me?"

"What about you? I think you were tailor-made for this job."

"Says you! Put 'em up!"

Rudy risked a glance down through the metal mesh of the fire escape just in time to see Bullet Head whip a pistol out of his overcoat and point it straight at Spiffy Dresser. Instead of "putting them up," Spiffy Dresser went for his own gun, and they stood aiming at each other and laughing as if they were doing a vaudeville act.

They held their weapons on each other all the way to the Packard, one chasing the other behind a row of garbage cans, the other chasing him out and forcing him onto the train tracks. When they finally got into the car and drove away through the snow, Isabel said, "They act like two little boys."

"Come on," Rudy said. "I gotta get in there and get them out."

Isabel nodded and led the way down the fire escape. To Rudy's surprise, there was no lock on the warehouse door, and they pushed their way in. Little Al and Hildy Helen grunted and squealed and snorted through their noses the moment they saw them. Gagged or not, it wasn't hard to know what they were saying.

"Took ya long enough, Rudolpho," Little Al said the instant Rudy pulled the dirty rag from his mouth. "This is the first time they've fed us, and I'm about to starve. The salami that thug just tried to feed me was about a hundred years old!"

"I don't know who you are," Hildy Helen said to Isabel, "but could you please untie me? My ankle hurts so bad."

Rudy did a hasty introduction and helped Isabel get them both untied. Little Al jumped right up and stamped his feet to get warm. But Hildy Helen couldn't even stand. Her ankle was swollen to twice its normal size and was bulging out of its bandage.

"You need a witch hazel compress and some Epsom salts," Isabel said.

"Yeah, well, first she needs to get outta here," Little Al said. "You say there's no lock on the door?"

"No," Rudy said. "But I'm gonna have to carry her. Look at that. She can't even take two steps."

"I can do it, Rudy," Hildy Helen said. "Just let me lean on you and Little Al, and I'll be fine."

But that method failed on the first attempt. The instant she put her weight on her ankle, Hildy Helen let out a scream that echoed through the warehouse.

"I told you she couldn't walk," Rudy said. He felt his stomach swirling into panic.

"So we both carry her," Little Al said, " 'cause as soon as they get a cuppa joe and get warmed up, those two mobsters are gonna be back."

"What is 'joe' anyway?" Hildy Helen said. Her face was blue-cold, and her teeth were clacking together, but Rudy saw that she was still trying to act as if everything were normal.

She must be braver than me, Rudy thought, *'cause I'm about to throw up! Jesus, please, where are You?*

"Joe is coffee," Isabel said. "I can help carry her."

"You go make sure the coast is clear," Little Al said. "This is a man's job."

So far Rudy hadn't seen anything a boy could do that Isabel couldn't, but this wasn't the time to argue with Little Al. Isabel slipped dutifully out the door, and Rudy and Little Al got on either side of Hildy Helen and made a seat for her with their arms. She slung her arms around their necks and said, "Let's go. I'll try to sit light."

It took a few strides for them to get in step with each other, but once they got the hang of it, the two boys sailed for the door with Hildy Helen clinging to their sleeves. It was only then that Rudy realized Little Al was still wearing only his tweed knickers and a pullover sweater. His face had an ashen look, while his hands were bright red and dried out as a pair of shriveled up old apples.

"Aren't you freezing?" Rudy said.

"I could use a cuppa joe myself," Little Al said. "Come on, we gotta beat it."

"Some of Quintonia's hot chocolate, that's what I want," Hildy Helen said.

Rudy could feel his throat tightening. That was going to happen. They were actually going to get home, all of them together, and they were going to drink hot cocoa and eat Christmas cookies and forget this ever happened.

But when they were only a few feet from the door, there was a rapping on the window above, by the fire escape.

"Somebody's coming!" Isabel said.

"Run!" Rudy said.

"No! They'll see you! Hide!" Isabel hissed, "Hide!" one more time before she disappeared from the window.

Rudy looked wildly at Little Al, who was whipping his head back and forth around the warehouse.

"Over there!" he said.

He pointed at a row of barrels against a far wall. With Hildy Helen still in their arms, they raced for it, weaving clumsily as they tried to propel themselves forward without dropping her. The barrels seemed to get farther away as the men's voices outside grew closer. Rudy tasted his lunch in his mouth as they dumped Hildy Helen behind the closest barrel and hid themselves behind the other two. He pressed his mitten to his lips to keep the lunch down and the breathing muffled. His whole body was racing like a Model T engine.

"Why didn't ya thinka coats 'n' blankets the first time? We shouldn'ta moved 'em to a place with no heat anyway," he heard Bullet Head say.

"Whatta we care if they freeze to death? They ain't our kids!"

The door came open, and Rudy could hear the wind howling. He hoped that would cover the sound of his heart drumming inside his chest.

"They ain't worth nothin' to the Boss if we let 'em freeze,"

Spiffy Dresser said. "And if they freeze, *we* ain't worth nothin' to the Boss. Hey!"

They'd spied the ropes, no longer tied around Hildy Helen and Little Al. Rudy squeezed his eyes shut, but he felt Little Al's hand on his arm. He looked at Al.

Al pointed to his eye and his chest. That was the signal for "watch me."

Rudy nodded and went back to holding his breath.

Most of the words the two men were shouting at each other, Rudy had never heard before. He figured it was a mixture of Italian and swearing, but it was obvious they were popping their veins with rage. Rudy kept his eyes on Little Al, who was squatted down on his toes as if he were ready to spring.

"We gotta find them!" Spiffy Dresser said.

"No kiddin'? Yer brilliant, Joey. Yer a regular Joe College. Of course we gotta find 'em. You check outside—"

"You check outside! I'm sicka that cold!"

"Whatta ya think it is in here, Palm Beach? Get out there!"

There was more Italian and more swearing. Rudy concentrated on praying. *Please, Jesus, let them* both *go outside!*

But when the front door slammed shut Bullet Head could still be heard ramming around inside the warehouse, cursing and throwing crates and boxes. Rudy stopped breathing altogether. The man was blazing a trail straight toward them.

Rudy looked at Little Al, but Al shook his head. *Not yet.* He was right; there was nowhere to run to now. Al pointed to Rudy and then in one direction, then to himself and in another. Rudy pointed to Hildy Helen. Little Al jabbed a thumb at himself. Rudy nodded.

I gotta lead Bullet Head away from them, Rudy told himself. *No matter what happens, I can't let 'em catch Hildy Helen again. Little Al will make sure she gets back to Quintonia's hot cocoa.*

Little Al gave him a jab in the ribs. Rudy shot out from the barrel, shouting for all he was worth. Behind him, he heard a barrel fall over, and Bullet Head gave a shout. Rudy looked back. Bullet Head was tripping over the barrel and trying to keep Rudy in his sight, so he didn't see Little Al with Hildy Helen on his back.

"Stop, ya little brat!" Bullet Head yelled at Rudy.

Rudy plowed across the warehouse, away from the door. He had to give Little Al and Hildy Helen time to get out. Then he could head for the entrance himself.

Tire this fella out, he kept thinking. *Keep running 'til he wears out.*

Rudy was sure he was going to wear *himself* out. Were they out yet? He didn't dare look toward the door for fear of giving them away. Bullet Head was still safely behind him, shouting curses. Just a little longer.

Then he heard the howl of the wind again, and he slowed down. *Let him think he can catch me, and he won't look at the door.*

But even as Bullet Head groped for him, Rudy heard another voice from the doorway. "Well, now, ain't this convenient? Ya walked right into my arms. Welcome home, kiddies!"

Rudy whipped his head toward the door. Spiffy Dresser stood at the door with Little Al caught by one arm, and Hildy Helen by the other.

Then a hand clutched the back of Rudy's collar, and he was shoved to the floor. A second later, Bullet Head dropped on top of him.

⚜ ⚜ ⚜

Chapter Fourteen

*J*oey and Bullet Head—whose name, Rudy heard, was Frankie—were much better at binding and gagging than they were at "baby-sitting." Within two minutes they had all three children tied up and their mouths stuffed with oily tasting rags. If Rudy had thought he'd felt sick before, he hadn't known the half of it.

"That oughta stop 'em," Frankie said. "They're not gonna get outta those anytime soon."

Rudy couldn't argue with that. He could feel the ropes cutting into his wrists and ankles, and he could barely breathe for the ones around his chest. It was a suffocating feeling.

"That one's turnin' blue, Frankie," Joey said, pointing to Hildy Helen. "I think ya got 'em too tight."

"Nah, she's just bellyachin' 'bout the cold. Here, I brought ya a blanket, girlie. Now no more kickin' about the cold, ya got it?"

Hildy Helen didn't give him her evil look this time. Rudy could see tears threatening to spill out. *Don't give up, Hildy Helen!* he thought. *Keep being brave! Pray!*

"And here's one for you, kid," Frankie said to Little Al as he dropped a blanket over him. "Sure beats me why one of our own would turn on us like this." He shook his finger at Little Al like

142

a scolding schoolteacher and then threw his head back and laughed. It had a wicked sound as it bounced off the warehouse walls. If Rudy hadn't been trembling already, it would have made him shiver.

"I suppose you want one, too," Frankie said. He was standing directly over Rudy, and even as Rudy looked up at him, recognition flickered through the tall man's eyes. "Hey!" he said. "Would ya looka here, Joey!"

"What's that?"

"It's the Hutchinson kid! The one we was out to nab in the first place!"

"Lucky for you," Joey said. "Since ya let him slip through your fingers the first two times."

"Hey, I slipped on the ice. And kids all look alike in the dark." He squatted down beside Rudy and held his face so close, Rudy could see the gold caps on his back teeth. "But yer not gonna get away this time, little Hutchie," he said. "So don't even try it."

In complete fear, Rudy tried to narrow his eyes at him, but Frankie wasn't cowed in the least. He gave another head-back laugh and straightened up. "Go tell the Boss, Joey," he said. "I'll stay here and watch these three."

"Sure, I don't mind givin' him good news."

"On second thought, let me tell him."

"You always gotta take all the glory! Why don't I ever get the glory?"

"Because yer too stupid to keep yer yap shut, that's why."

Frankie left. Joey continued to mutter under his breath. The only other sound was the wind swirling the snow outside the warehouse. Rudy closed his eyes and tried to think of something that would keep him from throwing up into his gag.

No drawings would come to his head. He didn't have any prayers either. He was all prayed out—and Jesus hadn't been answering anyway.

He groped for a hopeful thought, and he found only one. But it was enough to ease his lunch back down into his stomach.

Isabel was still out there somewhere. She'd gone for help, Rudy knew that for sure. Any time now, she'd be back with every policeman in the city.

If anyone would listen to her.

As it turned out, there was a prayer left, too. *Jesus, please let somebody listen to Isabel.*

Frankie returned shortly, puffed up with importance. "Boss says yer not supposed to leave 'em again, not even for a minute."

"What about you?" Joey growled.

"Me, too, but that ain't the thing."

"So what is the thing?"

"Boss says now that we got all three of 'em, thanks to me—"

"Thanks to us!"

"It's time to put the pressure on Jimmy Hutchinson." He kicked, none too gently, at the bottom of Rudy's foot. "We'll see how your old man stands up to the Boss now," he said.

"What pressure?" Joey said. "All he's gotta do is lay off the Levitsky case, and he gets his kids back. Simple as that."

"He won't do it!" Rudy wanted to scream at him. "Not once Isabel tells him what she knows!" *If only her father will let her talk to him,* he thought.

"What else did the Boss say?" Joey said.

"We gotta keep feedin' 'em and keepin' 'em warm. He said he doesn't want to give Jimmy Hutchinson damaged goods."

"He's a prince of a guy, the Boss is," Joey said. "You wanna know what I heard?"

"I probably heard it already."

"I heard tell the Boss helps any Italian comes to him off welfare."

"Oh, I knew that. He pays old people's hospital bills, sends their grandchildren to college." He grunted. "If he was watchin' these brats, he'd take 'em out for hot cocoa."

Huh, Rudy thought. *The same Al Capone that takes kids out for hot cocoa is the Al Capone that orders people pumped full of bullets.*

The thought of bullets stopped him for a minute. After all, they'd seen both hoods waving their guns around out in the snow.

But Rudy calmed that thought with the next one. *They aren't going to hurt us. We're all they have to get Dad to change his mind about helping the Levitskys.*

Frankie and Joey went on one-upping each other in what they knew about the Boss, and Rudy's mind drifted off.

Why was Al Capone's outfit so eager to ruin Uriah Levitsky? He had told Dad that they wanted him to buy their liquor. But what difference could the sales of one little grocery store possibly make to a rich man like Al Capone? What was that other thing they talked about? Protection money or something?

When Frankie had satisfied himself that he was far ahead of Joey in the study of Al Capone, he got up and said, "It's been a few hours. I guess we oughta feed these brats again."

He made Joey retrieve the food bags from the corner where he'd thrown them earlier and he himself got busy pulling the gags out of the children's mouths.

"You better eat this time, girlie," he said to Hildy Helen.

She didn't answer, and when Rudy looked at her, his stomach lurched. Her face was blotchy-blue against pasty white, and her eyes had none of their shine. She just sighed listlessly and turned her head away.

Little Al, on the other hand, didn't wait for Frankie to fill his mouth with food before he started spitting.

"If I had my way, I'd let you starve!" Frankie said. He wadded up a piece of bread and crammed it into Little Al's mouth, giving him no choice but to chew. Little Al did so with his eyes blazing.

Although Rudy's stomach was protesting at the very thought

of food, he obediently opened his mouth for the slice of bread Frankie offered him and chewed it like a grateful street urchin. Maybe the hoods would let down their guard if he co-operated.

"I wish we coulda just had this one all along," Frankie said to Joey. "At least he don't give us no lip."

"Why should I?" Rudy said, mouth full. "In a little while you're going to give us back to our dad, so why make a fuss?"

"Well, I'm certainly glad yer seein' things our way," Frankie said. "Here, lemme see if I can find ya a piece a salami that ain't green. Where'd you get this stuff, Joey?"

"You got it!" Joey said. "And I ain't feedin' the little one. I don't want him spittin' on my coat."

"So, you think if my father stops defending Levitsky, the old Jew'll start buyin' yer liquor?" Rudy said. "You'd stop killin' the Jews, then, right?"

Frankie grunted in Joey's direction. "We don't kill fer small-time liquor sales," he said.

"But you kill for somebody refusin' to pay protection money," Little Al said.

Rudy saw the gleam come back into Little Al's eyes. He knew what Rudy was trying to do. He should. He'd taught Rudy everything he knew about mobsters.

"Protection money?" Joey said. "Yeah, we kill over protection money—"

"But not this time," Frankie said. "Like I said, Levitsky's small-time. The Boss don't kill for small-time. He don't want trouble over somebody like that."

He looked smugly at Joey, as if he'd outdone him again.

"Then what's he out for this time, Mr. Smart Fella?" Joey said.

"Honor," Frankie said.

He was quiet for a moment, and Rudy watched his eyes take on a hardness that chilled Rudy right through his mackinaw coat. He was suddenly no longer the two-bit hood trying to out-Capone his friend. He was someone deadly cold who controlled the room with absolute hardness.

"We kill for honor," Frankie said. His voice matched his eyes now. "Boss says you gotta protect what you believe in. He don't want no trouble, but he ain't afraid of it either. The Boss does what he's gotta do. He tries to do it decent, but when scum like Levitsky don't cooperate, he don't care about decent no more."

"I heard him say it myself," Joey said, his voice straining to keep up. "He says, 'Joey, youse can get a lot more done with a kind word and a gun, than you can with a kind word alone.' He says that to me one day when we was—"

"You read that in the *Tribune*," Frankie said, cutting Joey off with a wave of his hand. He turned back to Rudy. "You tell yer old man that when ya get home, kid. You tell him the Boss don't give up. He might as well learn that right now if he don't want no more trouble. It could get worse next time."

Rudy stole another look at Hildy Helen. Her eyes were closed, and she was breathing so hard out of her mouth that her lips looked blown apart. He didn't see how it could get any worse.

"Hey, Rudy," Little Al said. "I figured something out."

"What?" Rudy said.

Little Al was looking hard at him. "Somebody put a piece of ice on the stage the night of the Christmas pageant. That's what Hildy Helen slipped on."

Rudy stared at him for a second. Why on earth was Little Al bringing that up now? Didn't they have bigger things to worry about than Maury Worthington?

Hildy Helen's over here turning blue, Rudy thought, *and you're still looking for revenge—*

But Little Al's eyes were still hard on him, and they didn't have the glint of revenge in them. They were trying to get a message to him. *Okay*, Rudy thought. *So you're telling me people slip and fall on ice—but we're inside! We don't have any ice!*

"All right, the party's over," Frankie said. "Time for yer gags again, kiddies. And then it's nighty-night time."

"Gee, Frankie, you run a pretty good nursery," Joey said.

Frankie paused with Little Al's gag midway to his mouth and glared at Joey.

"Hey, Frankie," Little Al said, "may I call ya Frankie?"

Frankie considered that with his head cocked. "No," he said, "it's Mr. LaPorte to you."

"All right, Mr. LaPorte, I'm thinkin' you might wanna fill up a glass a water for each of us before we go to sleep."

"I ain't no nursemaid!" Frankie said, glaring at Joey, who quickly did away with a smirk.

"This'll keep ya from bein' a nursemaid," Little Al said. "If we get thirsty in the middle a the night, we'll just grunt and you can take out our gags and pour it in. You won't have to go out to the pump or nothin'."

"Forget it," Joey said. "No drinks in the middle a the night."

"Jeepers," Little Al said. "Al Capone would be takin' us out for hot cocoa."

"Get three cups a water, Joey," Frankie said.

"In what?"

"There's three empty flasks in the car. Under the front seat."

Joey went out grumbling, and Frankie stuffed the gags into the kids' mouths. Rudy closed his eyes and tried to figure out why Little Al wanted them to have water. He'd never known his brother to wake up in the night for anything less than a full on-slaught on the house with a barrage of machine-gun fire.

When Joey returned with the flasks he'd filled with water, he set them, tops off, beside each of the children.

"What did ya take the caps off for?" Frankie said.

" 'Cause they're gonna taste like liquor if I don't," Joey said. "The Boss don't serve liquor to kids." He smiled smugly at

Frankie and went off to a corner of the warehouse. Rudy listened as Frankie followed him.

"Did ya bring enough blankets for us?" he said.

"No," Joey said.

"Whatsa matter, ya bohunk? Didn't you listen to the radio? It's gonna drop below zero tonight. That's cold enough to freeze beer, for cryin' out loud."

They argued for a few minutes, and then they lapsed into silence. A telltale snore told Rudy at least one of them had dozed off.

He whipped his head toward Al. He could see Little Al's eyes smiling as he moved his head over and carefully nudged with it at the bottle. The flask turned over and water spread into a puddle. Rudy grinned through his gag and did the same thing to his. That made two. Poor Hildy Helen was so sick—

But he heard still another flask go down. He looked at his sister. She looked at him listlessly and closed her eyes again.

I don't see how this is gonna work, Rudy thought. *They might fall, but they'll get right back up. We're tied up, for Pete's sake!*

But the gleam in Little Al's eyes meant he had something in mind. Rudy closed his eyes and tried to have faith.

As the night passed, Rudy was sure Frankie had been right about the temperature. He dozed off once, only to wake up to a sharp throbbing in his nose. His face was so cold he was afraid to move it for fear it would break. It was too dark to see Hildy Helen, but her breathing was hard and ragged, so he knew she must be asleep. He couldn't see whether he or Little Al had created icy patches with their water, but he prayed hard that they had. Once again, he drifted off.

He was awakened by a commotion on the other side of the warehouse. There was a light on, some kind of lantern, and he could hear Joey and Frankie talking.

"I tell ya, I heard somethin' out there."

"You were dreamin'."

"I wasn't even sleepin'. You were the one snorin' yer head off. The Boss don't like us sleepin' on the job."

"It came from up there, is what I say. From that window up there."

Rudy rolled himself to the side so he could see them. Frankie was holding the lantern up toward the window, the one Rudy and Isabel had peeked through from the fire escape. Rudy's heart started to hammer in his ears again.

Little Al was looking, too, and when Rudy heard a sound, he knew Little Al did, too. His head came up off the floor, just the way Rudy's did.

Rudy strained to hear past the hammering in his ears, and there it was again—the sound of stones being thrown against the window glass.

"Go out there," Frankie said.

Joey didn't argue this time. He headed straight for the door. The minute it closed behind him, Little Al cleared his throat. Rudy looked at him, and he did it again louder. His eyes were hard on Rudy.

When he cleared his throat again, Rudy coughed. Little Al's eyes smiled.

Rudy gave another hard cough and then fell into a coughing fit. It was tough with a rag stuffed in his mouth, but he made it sound as if he were dying of whooping cough.

Frankie looked his way, but turned back to the window with his lantern.

Beside him, Hildy Helen moaned. Rudy's stomach shivered, but when he looked at her, still coughing like a consumption patient, her eyes had a tiny flicker in them. It wasn't much—just enough to let him know she was faking it.

She moaned on and tried to talk, obviously to convince Frankie that she was writhing with pain.

It was pretty realistic as far as Rudy was concerned, but it didn't move Frankie. He didn't even look her way.

Only when Little Al gave a mighty heave and blew out his gag and yelled, "Hey, ugly! Over here!" did Frankie twirl on the heel of his pointy-toed shoe and nearly drop the lantern.

"Yeah, I'm talkin to you!" Little Al said. "Where'd you learn to put in a gag, huh? Yer nothin' but a two-bit thug, that's what I say!"

Frankie lost no time in heading toward Little Al, teeth bared. He didn't have to get much closer for Rudy to see that cold hardness in his eyes again.

I sure hope you know what you're doing, Little Al, Rudy thought.

"Shut up, ya little brat!" Frankie cried.

"Come over here and make me," Little Al said. "And see if you can do it right this time!"

It was more than Frankie's ego could bear. He set down the lantern and took the last two steps to Little Al with both arms outstretched.

But he never got there. One heel caught the icy patch, and Mr. LaPorte was flat on his back.

✢ ✛ ✢

Chapter Fifteen

*R*udy knew he was watching a miracle happen right before his eyes. Even before Frankie hit the floor, Little Al pulled his arms out of his ropes and wriggled the rest of himself free. Scrambling up, he flung his blanket over Frankie's head and wrapped his rope around him twice at the neck, tying it in a quick single knot.

"Get this off, ya brat!" Frankie screamed. "Or I'll kill ya!"

The menace in Frankie's voice was clear enough to freeze Rudy, but Little Al didn't seem to hear him. He moved over to Rudy and went to work on the knot in his rope. In seconds, Rudy's arms came free, but just then Frankie managed to struggle to his feet and started tearing at the blanket.

"You get the rest off!" Little Al said to Rudy. Then he stuck out his foot, and Frankie went down again.

By then, Rudy was out of his ropes and had pulled the gag from his mouth.

"Come on, help me!" Little Al said.

Hildy Helen was calling frantically from inside her gag, but Rudy did what Little Al said. If they didn't get this guy tied up someplace soon, it wasn't going to do much good to get her untied.

The last fall had obviously stunned Frankie, because he was moving slowly enough that Little Al and Rudy were able to wrap the rope around his ankles. He began to flail his arms weakly and curse, but Little Al and Rudy managed to get the last of the rope around his chest to keep his arms down. Finally, he was a muffled, screaming mass on the floor.

"Help me drag him," Little Al said.

"Where are we takin' him?"

Little Al gave a sharp jerk with his head toward a dark corner.

"What's over there?" Rudy said.

Little Al didn't answer. He just started dragging. Rudy struggled to pull on one arm while Little Al took the other. The mobster was fairly tall, but thankfully lean. From the way he was writhing and throwing himself around, Rudy knew he was mad, too. Rudy's heart was pounding up into his cheeks. If Frankie did get free, he wasn't going to care what his Boss wanted. It was his honor that was at stake now.

Little Al stopped in the corner, in front of something Rudy hadn't noticed before. There were two shovels leaning against what appeared to be a large bin. Its purpose was clear from the litter of coal that cluttered the floor.

"They got a coal furnace?" Rudy said as Little Al heaved Frankie's shoulders up onto the side of the bin.

"Yeah," Little Al said.

"Then why is it so cold in here?"

" 'Cause they were too stupid to use it!"

That provoked another torrent of curses from under the blanket, but Little Al knew how to shut those up, and now so did Rudy. Grinning at Little Al, Rudy hoisted Frankie's legs up and with a one-two-three from Little Al, they shoved the screaming mobster down into the coal bin.

"Can he get out?" Rudy said as they ran back across the warehouse toward Hildy Helen.

"Not for a while," Little Al said.

Just then, Rudy heard Joey yelling outside the door. "Frankie! We got trouble!"

"Come on," Little Al said.

When they got to Hildy Helen, Joey was still shouting outside. "Do we untie her?" Rudy said.

"No, we'll carry her this way."

Hildy Helen gave a moan of protest, but Little Al didn't even take the time to take her gag out. Once again, they gave it a one-two-three, picked her up, and carried her like a small log toward the back of the warehouse.

"How are we gonna get out?" Rudy said.

"While I was lyin' there, I was lookin' around," he said. "Just tonight I seen the garage door back here. Every warehouse has gotta have one, or how else are ya gonna get trucks in here?"

Little Al was right. There in the back of the warehouse was a garage door, just like the one on Aunt Gussie's garage, only bigger, of course. It was painted the same color as the back wall, so it had been easily camouflaged. Rudy was sure even Frankie and Joey hadn't seen it. With Frankie screaming in the coal bin those two were seeming stupider by the minute.

Suddenly, though, things changed. "Stop!" screeched Joey's voice behind them.

They didn't, though Rudy was sure his heart did.

"Stop! I gotta gun, and I'll use it on ya. Stop right there!"

Little Al glanced over his shoulder, and Rudy saw in his eyes that he had indeed seen the gun. Al stopped, but he didn't look scared. He had the same cold, hard look Rudy had seen on Frankie.

But Rudy was as frightened as he'd ever been in his life. He was so frozen that not even a thought would move in his head. Everything stood still—until from outside something began to wail, closer and closer, louder and louder, joined by other wails.

"It's the cops!" Little Al said.

Joey's head jerked to take a backward look. Little Al's foot came up and knocked the revolver out of Joey's hand. It landed on the floor next to Rudy's foot, and Rudy kicked it hard and watched it slide crazily across the warehouse floor and into the dark.

Joey cursed in Italian and dove for it. Little Al set down his half of Hildy Helen and yanked on the latch on the garage door. It gave an indignant screech, and Little Al shoved his body against the door. Behind him Rudy could hear Joey swearing and pounding with his hands, as if he could beat the gun out of that miserable floor.

"Gotcha!" Joey shouted suddenly.

While trying to hold on to his sister, Rudy let himself fall against the door, too. It creaked open a crack, and Little Al slithered out. Rudy stuffed Hildy Helen through and wriggled out after her.

"Grab her feet!" Little Al yelled.

"Stop right there!" yelled someone else inside the warehouse.

It wasn't Joey's voice this time. It had the snappish staccato of a Chicago policeman. *That should take care of Joey*, thought Rudy. And then another thought came to him.

"Run!" Rudy hissed. This was no time to trust people he wasn't certain were on their side.

He and Little Al took off running through the darkness, carrying Hildy Helen between them. Rudy wasn't sure when she'd gone limp, but she was harder to carry this way. He didn't know where they were going or how he was going to hold on to her much longer, but the boys kept running, knees lifting high in the snow.

"Stop—or I'll shoot!" another rapid-fire voice spat out at them.

"No, those are my children!"

"That's Dad!" Rudy cried. "Little Al, that's Dad!"

Little Al stopped, and they turned around. A policeman's torch hit them full in the face with its glaring light.

"Dad!" Rudy shouted. "Dad, the cops are after us!"

Another second and he was collapsed against his father, smashed into the front of his overcoat by Little Al and Hildy Helen. Dad held them, and Rudy could feel his chest giving big, labored heaves. The policeman stood over them, shining the torch down.

Suddenly Dad let the boys go and scooped Hildy Helen up. Her head sagged over his arm.

"Ambulance!" he called out. "We need that ambulance over here!"

By the time the attendants got Hildy Helen onto a stretcher, she was awake again and begging to be taken home and not to the hospital.

"We're just going to have you checked out," Dad said. "You, too, Al, and no arguments."

Little Al climbed into the back of the ambulance with her, but only under protest—and only with the promise that Dad would follow soon with Rudy in the car. Then he stood and watched grimly as the police stuffed Frankie and Joey into a police car.

"Rudy," he said, "we have to find Isabel."

"Isabel?" Rudy said. "I thought she was with you. Didn't she bring you here?"

Dad put his arm around Rudy and pulled him with him as he set off across the warehouse yard, scanning it with his eyes.

"She went straight home to tell her father," he said, "but Uriah wouldn't listen to her. He was too angry at her for taking off like that."

"He never listens to her!" Rudy said.

"Thank the good Lord I arrived just as he was sending her to her room. The poor child looked so upset, I talked him into letting her tell her story. As soon as she told us where you all were, I called the police and told them I'd meet them here. She wanted to come with me—" Dad shook his head as he continued his search of the yard with his eyes. "But I didn't listen to her either. I told her it was too dangerous and that the police would handle everything. She just bolted out of the store and took off. I thought for sure she'd come back here."

"She did," Rudy said. "She threw stones against the window and got those mobsters' attention away from us so Little Al could make his plan work. You can't trust the police, you know, Dad."

His father gave him a curious look, but he blinked and said, "Let's find Isabel before we get into that. Any idea where she might be?"

Rudy's eyes flew up to the fire escape, and there was a chunky little form curled up on the step—away from the cold, out of everyone's sight, out of everyone's mind.

"Right there," Rudy said. "I'll get her."

But Dad wasn't letting Rudy out of his sight. He followed him up the fire escape and sat on the step below Isabel. Her teeth were chattering, and her chin was quivering.

"Where's your coat?" Rudy said.

"I didn't have time to get it," she said. Her words were broken like pieces of ice, and her shoulders shuddered in the cold.

Dad whipped off his overcoat and wrapped it around her. Rudy put his mittens on her and shoved his own hands into his pockets. Dad carried her to the Pierce Arrow, and they sat in the front seat with her between them. Dad rubbed her hands together inside the mittens and let the car's heater blast at her until her shoulders stopped shaking.

"You children are determined to get frostbite, aren't you?" Dad said. He smiled at Isabel, but she looked at Rudy.

"Is now a good time to tell him about the Italian boys?" she said. "Do you think he'll listen?"

Dad pulled her into a hug and smiled at Rudy over her head. "Will I listen?" he said. "Such a question. I'll listen, all right."

So Isabel told her story to Jim Hutchinson as they rode to the hospital. When they pulled up to the curb, Dad turned off the engine and looked down at her.

"Would you tell that to the police, Isabel?" he said.

"Not the police, Dad. They're in on it!" Rudy insisted.

Once again, Dad looked curiously at Rudy. "Some of them are, I know that," he said. He turned to Isabel, "I promise you will be protected."

"But how could that help?" Isabel said. "No one's going to listen to a Jewish girl. Can't you just tell my story? Can't Rudy tell it?"

"You're the witness," Dad said. "The only problem I see is that they'll think you're lying to protect your brother." He patted Isabel's hand. "But I'll find some way to use this information, don't you worry. You've done a great deal to help your brother tonight—not to mention my children. We owe you their lives. I'll never forget that."

Hildy Helen was already looking a little pinker and more cheerful when they got to her in the hospital. She was drinking hot cocoa while a young doctor with Rudy Vallee hair was wrapping her ankle. She was halfway to seventh heaven.

And Little Al? He was sitting on the edge of an examining table, swinging his legs and telling their whole tale to a nurse who was trying unsuccessfully to get a look down his throat.

"Hey," he said as Rudy and his father walked in, "have I told you I like a doll like you?"

"Don't believe a word of it," Dad said. "He says that to all the girls."

"Now *that* I believe," the nurse said. She ruffled Al's hair and left. Little Al scowled after her.

"She didn't have to mess up my hair," he said. "You gotta mirror, Rudy?"

"Never mind that," Dad said. "The police are going to ask you some questions as soon as the doctor says you can go."

"Not the police!" Rudy said. "We don't know if we can trust them!"

Dad squinted at him through his glasses. "What is this, Rudy? Why do you keep telling me I can't count on the police?"

"Because," Rudy said, and then he spilled out what he'd heard at the station about Al Capone.

Dad considered it for a moment, and then he seemed to set it aside. "All I know is," he said, "we can count on Detective Zorn."

"But how do you know?"

"Because I've gotten to know him," Dad said. "We can't say all policemen are crooked. We have to get to know each one individually."

Something about that went through Rudy.

Dad turned to Little Al. "Before I turn you loose on the police, I have a couple of questions of my own first."

"Shoot, Mr. Hutchie."

"Why did you leave the house to go looking for Hildy Helen when I expressly told you not to? And don't tell me it's a good thing you did because you helped rescue her. That isn't the point—"

"But I didn't leave the house, Mr. Hutchie," Little Al said. "At least, not on my own. I went upstairs to mope because you wouldn't let me out. And the next thing I know, Frankie LaPorte steps outta the wardrobe and shoves a gag in my mouth. It musta had somethin' on it, 'cause that's the last thing I remember 'til I woke up in that warehouse beside Hildy Helen."

"That's true, Dad," Rudy said. "Frankie and Joey, they were talking about it. They were supposed to kidnap me—only I was asleep in Hildy Helen's room that night."

"Mr. Hutchinson?" the nurse said, peeking around the curtain. "There's a Mr. Levitsky here to see you."

Dad nodded and went out through the curtain.

"I got a question, too," Rudy said to Little Al. "How did you get out of those ropes so easy?"

"Simple," Little Al said. "That last time they tied the ropes round my middle, I filled myself all fulla air, the way I did when they were measurin' me for my costume pants so they'd hang like Oxford bags. Then when they had the ropes on, I let the air out, and there was room to get my arms outta there." He grinned. "I thought I was gonna pass out, though, holdin' my breath for that long."

The curtain pulled open. "Rudy?" Dad said. "Could you come out here for a minute, please?"

Rudy stepped outside the curtain. Uriah Levitsky was there, standing next to a white-faced Isabel. He was plucking his beard, and his eyes were smoldering. From the looks of Isabel, Rudy knew she was expecting to catch the fire from those eyes as soon as they left the hospital.

"Rudy," Dad said, "would you tell Mr. Levitsky what Isabel did tonight?"

Rudy looked quickly at Isabel, but she wasn't begging him with her eyes the way he would have been doing. She just hung her head toward the floor.

"I'm not gonna rat on her, if that's what you mean," Rudy said. "I don't rat on friends—even if they *are* Jewish."

The words were out before he could stop them. They brought Isabel's head up, and sent Uriah's eyebrows down over his eyes.

"Friend?" Uriah said. "She's a friend all right—dragging you into places she didn't belong, poking her nose into business that wasn't her own. Always the poking with her, yah."

"It wasn't like that," Rudy said. "She's the only reason Little Al and Hildy Helen got free! If it hadn't been for her, I'd have messed up the whole thing. I know I would! I'm not good at this stuff; she is." Rudy's heart was hammering again, and he could barely catch his breath. "She's brave, and she thinks fast, and she hears things adults don't hear and sees things adults don't see, because she knows how to listen. And you—you oughta—"

Rudy bit his lip. That was going too far, to tell Isabel's father how he ought to treat her. But he wanted him to know.

"Rudy listened to Isabel because she's a smart girl, Uriah," Dad said. "I'm not one to poke my nose in where it doesn't belong, but this time I'm going to make an exception. She's a good girl. You should listen to her."

Uriah scowled.

"You'll be sorry if you don't," Dad said. "Because right now, she's the only one who can set Nathaniel free."

"Ach, the promises!" Uriah cried. "Always the promises with you!"

"Hear me out," Dad said.

He led Mr. Levitsky away from the possibly unseen ears of the examining area and down the hall, where he talked to him in a low voice. Rudy stole a glance at Isabel. She was driving her eyes right into him.

"What?" he said. "Sometimes you give me the heebie-jeebies when you look at me like that, Isabel."

"Did you really mean it when you said I was your friend?" she said.

"I don't know," Rudy said. "I guess." He was feeling confused. "Look, I stuck up for you with your dad, didn't I?" He looked down the hall. "Your dad's already smiling. You're not gonna get a licking when you get home, thanks to me and my dad."

As he started to look back at Isabel, his eye caught on a shiny light, just beyond where his father and Uriah were talking. It was several lights, actually, twinkling on a pitiful-looking little Christmas tree perched on a shelf. It gave him an idea.

"You and your family come to our house on Christmas Eve for a party we're having," Rudy said.

"Christmas?" she said.

"I came to your place for Hanukkah, didn't I?" Rudy said.

Isabel gave him another one of those long looks. Rudy tried to wait it out.

"I don't know," she said finally.

"Why not?"

"Because—I've always thought, if God doesn't like gentiles, why should I?"

"Oh," Rudy said. He shoved his hands into his pockets. "Well, if you come, you come. And if you don't, you don't."

She didn't answer. She just hurried off down the hall as her father barked for her. Rudy suddenly felt hollow with disappointment.

What do I care if she comes over or not? he thought. *I just said that to have something to talk about.*

But another thought skipped through his mind, and this one surprised him even more.

She didn't even seem that funny-looking to me tonight, he thought. *Even if she is a Jew.*

✠ ⚜ ✠

Chapter Sixteen

*I*t stopped snowing by Christmas Eve, and the sky was a bright, endless blue outside the parlor where the three children were hanging up their stockings on the mantel.

Actually, Little Al and Rudy were hanging the stockings. Hildy Helen was giving instructions from the sofa, while drinking her third cup of hot cocoa. Quintonia had planted Hildy there with her foot up on a pillow with orders not to move or she'd be "hung up with them socks."

"Put mine in the center," Hildy Helen said now.

Rudy dutifully pulled the stool shaped like a crocodile to the center of the fireplace and stepped up on it. He was about to hook the stocking from the trunk of a large ivory elephant when she said, "No, I think it would look better on the end, since yours and mine are the same and Little Al's is different. His should be in the center."

Rudy frowned at Little Al.

"Dames are always changin' their minds, Rudolpho," Little Al said, as Rudy stepped down once more and moved the stool. "You oughta know that by now."

Rudy just shrugged. It didn't really matter to him if they hung the stockings outside on the clothesline. He hadn't been in a

Christmas mood since the rescue—at least, not the way he had before all the trouble. Rudy still had that hollow of disappointment he'd felt when Isabel had walked away from him at the hospital.

In the first place, Aunt Gussie had been in bed ever since the night Hildy Helen and Little Al had disappeared. Even Quintonia had barely been able to get her to eat, and only when Dad had carried Hildy Helen into her room with Little Al trailing behind had she lifted her head. But even since then, the orders had been for quiet. Aunt Gussie still wasn't strong. Dad had told them that for the first time in 40 years, she wasn't going to be able to have her Christmas Eve party. Besides that, Rudy had also heard Dad and Dr. Kennedy talking about how perhaps Aunt Gussie should move out of this neighborhood, to someplace calmer, someplace that would be easier to take care of. That was when the hollow had begun to dig itself deeper inside Rudy.

And then Dad had been working almost from the moment he'd brought them home, still trying to do something for Nathaniel. "I want him out of that jail," Dad had told the kids. "What the DA does about Isabel's testimony will decide that."

Besides that, Bridget and Sol weren't there. Sol was still recovering from being hit on the head, and Bridget refused to leave him. She seemed to be the only person Sol remembered.

Rudy missed the old chauffeur's grunts and one-syllable answers. Riding in the Pierce Arrow just wouldn't be the same without him at the wheel. It would be hard to open presents Christmas morning without Bridget and her silvery laugh, too.

The house was still filled with the cinnamon and nutmeg smells that wafted out of the kitchen, and Christmas carol sounds came from the music room whenever Little Al was in there practicing his violin. But Rudy was more interested in the sound of the phone than in any of that. Every time it rang he ran to it. But it was never Isabel saying she'd come. He hadn't figured out why he wanted her there so much, but if she didn't show up, something else was going to be missing.

"Wait!" Hildy said suddenly, sitting up straight on the sofa. "Put yours in the middle, Rudy. You're the oldest. You should be in the middle."

"I'll tell you where I'm gonna hang it," Rudy said through his teeth. "Right from the end of your nose!"

"Now what kind of talk is that for Christmas Eve?" said a voice from the doorway.

Rudy whirled around and stumbled off the stool. It was Aunt Gussie, or at least a woman who looked something like her. Her face was pale, and the dark green silk she wore seemed to hang on the rather limp form of the usually robust Gustavia Nitz.

But what shocked Rudy was the walking stick she leaned on as she took a step into the room.

"Don't tell Quintonia I'm out here," she said in a loud whisper. "She'll come after me with a thermometer or something."

"I know just how you feel, Aunt Gussie," Hildy Helen said. "She thinks I'm an invalid."

"Well, *I'm* certainly not one," Aunt Gussie said. She took a few more steps across the parlor, thumping the stick as she went. Rudy couldn't take his eyes from it. It turned her into a stranger. Aunt Gussie was a person who marched around the house like a general, bringing everything she passed to attention. This was an old woman with a cane who was barely making it to the sofa.

"Let me make a place for you, Auntie," Hildy Helen said, sliding her foot out of the way so Aunt Gussie could sink down onto the horsehair couch beside her. Aunt Gussie did so with what sounded like a grateful sigh.

Little Al moved the crocodile stool over to her and ceremoniously propped her feet on it. "So, Miss Gustavio," he said, "what's with the crutch?"

Aunt Gussie waved it at him as if to dismiss the matter. "Dr.

Kennedy says I had a small stroke when you two children were kidnapped. He tried to tell me I'll have a game leg for the rest of my days." She sniffed. "I told him he was full of soup. I intend to discard this thing by the time Hildy Helen is back up and around."

"We'll have a contest!" Hildy Helen said, grinning.

"Careful, now," Aunt Gussie said. "I know how you hate to lose."

"I do not! I'm a good sport!"

"Ah, and that would be why on the very night of your capture, you were pouting because you were running dead last in mah jongg."

Rudy felt his shoulders relax a little. Maybe it was still Aunt Gussie after all.

"I'm glad I came out here when I did," she said, looking up at the mantel. "Whoever hung those stockings has them all wrong."

"I told them that," Hildy Helen said. "But did they listen to me?"

"Yes!" Rudy and Little Al said at the same time.

"Where are Quintonia's and your father's, not to mention Bridget's and Sol's?"

"Bridget and Sol?" Rudy said. "But they aren't going to be here."

"And why in heaven's name not? Your father has gone to get them both from the hospital. We're going to have to bring another couch in here for all the infirmary patients."

Rudy began to feel a little less empty. But it still wasn't enough to be a complete Christmas.

"Why did Bridget stay at the hospital with Sol that whole time?" Hildy Helen said.

"Because the Spirit moved her, I think," Aunt Gussie said. "Jesus is very proud of her, I would say."

Then she gave each of the children a look so long, Rudy thought she might be having another stroke, whatever that was.

Finally she said, "I think there are a lot of people Jesus is proud of in this house. Quintonia, who refused to let me slip away. Your father, who is knocking himself out working for the Levitsky boy, and refusing to knuckle under to those mobsters." A faint smile crossed her face. "You children for getting yourselves out of the clutches of those vicious animals—"

She stopped, and Rudy saw that the rims of her eyes were red.

"I prayed to the Lord while I was lying there," she went on. "I was so angry with your father for putting his family in such danger. If he had just given up this case. And then I let the Lord speak to me, and He said, 'Gustavia, I'm proud of James. Let him do what I sent him here to do. I will take care of his family. I will show him a way to help the Levitskys. Don't you stand in his way.'"

"The Lord really talks to you, Aunt Gussie?" Hildy Helen said.

But Rudy cut her off. "The Lord said He was gonna help the Levitskys?"

"Yes."

"But I don't understand."

"Why, Rudolph?"

"Because," Rudy said, "well, they're Jewish."

The words didn't roll right off his lips this time though. And when they were out there in the parlor air, mixed with the smell of cinnamon and nutmeg, they somehow made as little sense to him as the squiggles on a Yiddish sign.

"Hmm," Aunt Gussie said. She crossed her hands on the top of the walking stick and rested her chin on them. "We shall have to see about that—perhaps tonight at our party."

"Party?" Hildy Helen said.

"I thought we weren't havin' no party, on a counta yer bein' laid up," Little Al said.

"Nonsense," Aunt Gussie said. "I told Quintonia and your father this morning, there will be a party or no one around here gets a thing for Christmas." She twitched an eyebrow at their stricken looks. "There will be a party—a smaller one than usual, of course. But we have to celebrate. It's Jesus' birthday, after all!"

"Right you are, Miss Gustavio!" Little Al said.

"However, that does bring one thing to mind." She pursed her lips at the children. "You haven't forgotten my instructions, have you?"

"What instructions?" Rudy said.

"You are to give each other something Jesus would be proud of."

Rudy watched as Little Al's and Hildy Helen's faces fell—and he knew his would be the first to hit the ground.

"But Aunt Gussie!" Hildy Helen said. "Everything happened so fast, we didn't have time to go shopping—"

"There is no need for shopping," Aunt Gussie said. "I think you'll find everything you need right in your hearts."

She took a deep breath then and got herself to her feet. She was leaning even more heavily on the cane now, and her face was losing its color.

"I'd better get back to my room before Quintonia finds me," she said.

"Hey, Miss Gustavio, before you go," Little Al said. "I gotta tell you somethin'."

"Yes, Alonzo?"

"I just gotta say, I like a doll with a walkin' stick."

Aunt Gussie closed her eyes, and when she opened them, they were wet. "Thank you, Alonzo," she said. "And you can go ahead and check me off your list. I just received my gift from you."

When she was gone, they finished the stockings to Hildy's satisfaction, finally. When Quintonia came in with still another tray of hot cocoa, Rudy excused himself and went upstairs. The hollow inside was getting deeper again.

There was only one thing to do, and that was to draw. He had to make presents for Hildy Helen and Little Al anyway.

But before he could even pick up his pencil, his mind began to race.

I thought I had this gift thing all wrapped up, he thought. *I was just gonna scratch out a drawing for everybody because I thought I had this gift. Because I thought I was some big-shot Christian.*

His own thoughts stunned him, and they made him feel even more disappointed. This time it was himself he was disappointed in.

I think I was . . . I think I was conceited, he thought. *No wonder I'm not hearing answers anymore. Jesus isn't proud of me. He's disappointed in me.*

Now I don't know what to do.

He looked down at the sketch pad, strangely empty in front of him.

But I'm a Christian! he thought. *Why wouldn't He be proud of me?*

Rudy closed his eyes to the answer, but it came anyway.

What about the way he'd treated Isabel? What about the things he'd said to Nathaniel? What about the way his head had gotten all full of revenge against Maury Worthington?

He couldn't seem to sort it out. It all just got thrown into a heap inside his mind, where it landed on something else. *I wasn't a good Christian all the time*, he realized. *Does Jesus love me now? And Isabel and Nathaniel, they're good people. Does God really not love them because they're Jewish?*

His throat got tight.

I don't know, Jesus, he thought. *You tell me what to draw, all right? I think I'm too mixed up.*

For a minute he thought he was actually going to cry.

I gotta do something, he thought, blinking his eyes frantically. *Please, Jesus, help, even though I probably don't deserve it.*

After a minute, he picked up his pencil. If he wasn't going to get an answer, he'd have to do it on his own. What would Jesus be proud of?

Well, he thought as he bit at his pencil, *Jesus is probably really proud of Hildy Helen and Little Al. They don't walk around like they're big-shot Christians—not like I do.*

His pencil began to sketch. Hildy Helen appeared, and so did Little Al. They were playing with a dreidel. And then Isabel appeared—and Nathaniel, too. They all had smiles on their comically drawn faces.

As Rudy rolled up the drawing and tied a piece of string around it, he felt a deep longing inside that hollow. *I wish I were in that picture*, he thought. *But I don't think I fit with them.* No wonder it didn't feel like Christmas.

But their guests began arriving that evening just the same, and each ring of the doorbell was a surprise, since no one but Aunt Gussie knew who had actually been invited.

Judge Caduff came in with his meaty hands full of fruitcakes and packages. Dad was next with Bridget and Sol. Robert McCormick, the "Colonel," arrived with early editions of the *Tribune* that no one else in the city had seen.

"It's like getting a peek at the future!" Bridget said.

"Look at the real estate ads, Gussie," Colonel McCormick said. "I tell you, it's time you moved out of this neighborhood. I should think all the trouble you've just had would be plenty of evidence."

"I will not discuss leaving this house, Robert," she said primly. "Now have a rum log and hush up about it."

Rudy gave a long sigh. At least that was one thing he didn't have to worry about anymore.

Then came Dr. Kennedy, who examined each of his three patients in the parlor and declared them all fit to celebrate. Personally, Rudy thought Sol was deafer than ever, but he sat with a half-grin on his face all evening. Rudy was convinced he was remembering something.

Miss Tibbs was the next to arrive. Rudy had a hard time looking at her. After all, the last time they'd talked, she had been pretty disappointed in Rudy.

But Miss Tibbs had no trouble looking at him. As soon as Dad had taken her coat, she walked right over to Rudy and said, "I understand you're a hero."

Rudy shrugged and looked at the floor.

"Rudy," she said. She pulled up his face by the chin. "You were brave to go after Hildy Helen and to help Isabel. You may have your silly seasons, Rudy Hutchinson, but you're certainly tops in my book."

Fortunately, Rudy didn't have a chance to answer, because his father came and led Miss Tibbs off by the elbow. Suddenly it looked as if there wasn't anyone else in the place, as far as Miss Tibbs was concerned. All three of the children immediately sent their antennae up to watch for telltale signs of romance between her and Dad. Later, when Hildy Helen reported having seen them both looking longingly up at the mistletoe, she declared that they were indeed "stuck on each other."

Rudy's attention, however, kept wandering back to the front door, and several times he went to the library window to look out.

Aunt Gussie probably didn't invite them, he kept telling himself. *Or maybe they don't want to be with us on our holiday any more than I wanted to be with them on theirs. It's probably what I deserve for being so stuck-up.*

Finally he gave up and went back to the parlor, where Dad was just beginning a Christmas toast with Quintonia's special punch. Rudy picked up a cup and thought to himself, *Here's to you, Isabel. Merry Christmas. Happy Hanukkah.*

"To all of God's many, many blessings," Dad was saying. "Not the least of which are our families and friends."

"Yah, friends are a blessing, all right!"

Rudy's punch sloshed over the rim of his cup.

"Uriah!" Dad said, smiling. "I'd almost given up on you!"

Uriah Levitsky smiled from the parlor doorway, and beside him stood his wife, her mouth in its usual straight line, her eyes shy amid a roomful of strangers.

But Rudy's eyes went past her and searched the doorway behind her.

Sure enough, there was Isabel, dressed in brown velvet and studying the floor.

Rudy put down his cup and went straight to her. "Hey," he said.

She looked up, and her eyes pointed into him.

He shrugged. "This is where I live."

"Oh," she said.

Rudy dug a toe into the rug and then said, "Want to meet my sister?"

Her face lit up like a menorah candle, and the emptiness inside of Rudy almost completely disappeared.

They were no sooner settled on the couch with Hildy Helen than Aunt Gussie held up her hand from the couch she was sharing with Sol. The room, of course, came to attention.

"Everyone has met the Levitskys?" she said.

There was a round of nods.

"I am so glad you were able to join us," Aunt Gussie said to Uriah and his wife, who still stood somewhat stiffly by the piano with plates of fruitcake in their hands. *They probably don't like it*, Rudy thought. *It isn't as good as* rugalach.

"I have been doing some studying about the Jewish faith since James began to work for you," Aunt Gussie said, "and I have discovered something I never noticed before."

Uriah nodded solemnly and toyed with his beard. Rudy swallowed. He sure hoped Aunt Gussie wasn't going to hurt Isabel's feelings.

"Jesus," she said, "was not only a Jew, but He came from 42 generations of Jews."

"You don't say," Robert McCormick said. "How do you figure that?"

"Read it for yourself, Colonel," Aunt Gussie said, peering at him over her glasses. "It's right there at the beginning of the book of Matthew."

"You're not talking about all those 'begats'?"

"I am indeed. So you see, anyone who thinks a Jewish person is worth less than a Christian is insulting Jesus Himself."

Rudy blushed. He could feel Isabel straightening beside him. She was now pointing her intense little eyes at Aunt Gussie.

"Now, in our faith," Aunt Gussie said, pressing her hand to her chest, "we believe that Jesus came to fulfill the promises that God had made to the Jews." She nodded at Quintonia, who slipped into the dining room and reappeared with a candleholder with nine candles. Rudy heard Isabel give a soft little gasp.

"This is my part in promoting our respect for each other," Aunt Gussie said. She nodded at Uriah. "Will you do us the honor of lighting this, Mr. Levitsky? After all, we are both remembering the wonderful works of the God of Isaac and Jacob."

It grew so silent in the room that Rudy could hear his own breath whistling through his nostrils. He didn't dare move, didn't dare look at Uriah Levitsky. If he were going to gather up his family and leave, Rudy didn't want to watch them go. Why should they honor this, after the way Rudy had treated their Hanukkah? The disappointment cut a deeper hole in him.

"Ah—such a question!" Uriah said suddenly. He looked at his

wife, his eyes glistening. His voice was soft. "God's works *are* wonderful, yah?"

And then Uriah smiled through his beard. He held his punch cup above his head. "To the God of Isaac and Jacob!"

The room burst into a relieved, "To the God of Isaac and Jacob!"

Uriah lit the candles, and once more the glow of the light made everyone in the room look alike. A quiet voice beside Rudy said, "If God likes gentiles, I guess I do, too."

Rudy turned to look at Isabel. She was blinking expectantly.

"Sure," Rudy said. "Me, too—you know, about Jews."

Then he shrugged, and she looked at the floor, and Rudy wished somebody would tell a joke. But at least now—suddenly— it felt like Christmas again.

From then on, the room seemed to take on a party sparkle. Colonel McCormick told tales of his adventures on the streets of Chicago gathering stories. In the midst of one of them, he looked at Uriah Levitsky and said, "I think the *Tribune* should stand behind your son. I'd like to interview you later. Don't you think that's a good idea, Jim?"

There was no answer, and everyone looked around the room.

"Where did he get to?" the colonel said.

Little Al peered out the window, and Rudy went out in the hall to check out the library. Miss Tibbs seemed to be missing, too, and that gave him the heebie-jeebies.

Rudy was just peeking out through the library drapes to investigate the front yard when he saw three figures hurrying up to the front porch. It was Dad with Miss Tibbs, all right. But who was that other person? A thin young man—

Rudy tore for the front door, screaming, "Isabel! Isabel, come here!"

They nearly collided in the front hallway. Rudy grabbed her sleeve and dragged her to the door, which was just opening to let in an invigorating blast of Christmas Eve air, along with Dad and Miss Tibbs—and Nathaniel Levitsky.

Isabel let out a scream that brought everyone in from the parlor, leaving Hildy Helen squalling from her couch, "Hey, what about me?"

When Uriah Levitsky saw his son, a stream of Yiddish flowed from his lips, and he began to cry. It wasn't an embarrassing kind of crying. Even Rudy didn't look at the floor and dig his toe into the rug.

"How in the world did you pull this off?" Robert McCormick said to Dad.

Judge Caduff put a big, beefy hand on Dad's shoulder. "When James Hutchinson puts his mind to something, between his efforts and the Lord's intervention, it usually happens."

"The DA finally made his decision," Dad said. "He isn't going after the real shooter, mind you. He's far too afraid of the mob for that. But after going over Isabel's deposition until he was blue in the face, he dropped the charges against Nathaniel."

"What's a deposition?" Hildy Helen said from her perch on Little Al's back.

"It's a special statement made in the district attorney's office," Dad said.

Rudy stared at Isabel. "You did that?" he said. "Weren't you scared?"

"No," she said. "He listened to me." Then she smiled and added, "And Papa was with me."

Uriah turned to Dad with the tears running shamelessly down into his beard. "This is a gift, Mr. Jim—Christmas, Hanukkah—it is a gift from the heart."

"Something Jesus would be proud of," Aunt Gussie said.

Rudy thought about the rolled-up drawing upstairs. He was still going to give it to Hildy Helen and Little Al, maybe tomorrow. But suddenly he knew what he was going to give them tonight, when it was time for the Jesus gifts.

It was very late when everyone left. Hildy Helen, Little Al, and Rudy all climbed onto Rudy's bed. There was no going to sleep, not with all those gifts piled up under the tree and the smell of cinnamon and cocoa and Little Al's longed-for cannoli still in the air. They launched into speculating whether Hildy Helen's wind-up Victrola was that very minute being wrapped and how many pairs of Oxford bags Little Al was going to add to his wardrobe, along with the shiny silver yo-yo. Then Rudy said, "It's time to give each other our Jesus gifts."

"I just didn't know what that meant," Hildy Helen said, her voice going up into a whine. "I guess Jesus isn't very proud of me."

"You better start, Rudolpho," Little Al said. "I think you must know Jesus better than any of us."

Rudy sat up and looked down at Little Al. "I don't want us to find Maury Worthington's house and get back at him for Hildy Helen," he said. "I think since God loves him—even if he's a Jew—we gotta—"

"Don't tell me I gotta love him!" Little Al said.

"Well, to start with," Rudy said, "we at least gotta stop the war with him."

Little Al frowned in the dark. "So what's my gift?"

"I'm gonna help you make friends with him," Rudy said. "I don't know how I'm gonna do it, but so far we've figured everything out, right?"

Little Al pondered that for a minute, and Rudy wasn't sure that gift wouldn't come flying back into his face.

But finally Little Al grinned. "You know, Rudolpho, I like a fella like you."

"What about me?" Hildy Helen said, tugging at Rudy's pajama sleeve.

"Well," Rudy said slowly, "all the time when we're doing stuff together, you and me and Little Al, it's always two boys and one girl."

"I know," she said, pulling her mouth into a prune. "Sometimes I get so mad—"

"So you won't have to anymore," Rudy said, "because I'm giving you a friend."

"Is it that Isabel girl?" Hildy Helen said.

"Um—"

"Say it is, Rudy! I like her. She's spunky!"

"Yeah, it's her."

"Of course, she isn't very modern," Hildy Helen said, "but we could work on that. Do you think her mother would let her get her hair bobbed?"

Little Al rolled his eyes. "Does everyone in the world gotta have their hair bobbed to make you happy?"

As Little Al gave Hildy Helen the business and she gave it right back, Rudy slid back down onto the bed and waited for them to give him his gifts Jesus could be proud of.

Of course, he thought as his eyes grew heavy, *I don't really need anything*.

His brother and sister were here, and they were safe. Downstairs, his father and Aunt Gussie were piling more presents under the tree.

And on the dining room table, next to the manger scene, there was a menorah.

He's the Light of the world, Rudy thought sleepily. He hoped the Levitskys would see it that way someday. Because God loved them as much as He loved anybody. *And I guess I do, too*, he thought.

And that, he decided, was something Jesus would be proud of.

✝-✞-✝

There's More Adventure in the CHRISTIAN HERITAGE SERIES!

The Salem Years, 1689–1691

The Rescue #1

Josiah Hutchinson's sister Hope is terribly ill. Can a stranger—whose presence could destroy the family's relationship with everyone else in Salem Village—save her?

The Stowaway #2

Josiah's dream of becoming a sailor seems within reach. But will the evil schemes of a tough orphan named Simon land Josiah and his sister in a heap of trouble?

The Guardian #3

Josiah has a plan to deal with the wolves threatening the town. Can he carry it out without endangering himself—or Cousin Rebecca, who'll follow him anywhere?

The Accused #4

Robbed by the cruel Putnam brothers, Josiah suddenly finds himself on trial for crimes he didn't commit. Can he convince anyone of his innocence?

The Samaritan #5

Josiah tries to help a starving widow and her daughter. But will his feud with the Putnams wreck everything he's worked for?

The Secret #6

If Papa finds out who Hope's been sneaking away to see, he'll be furious! Josiah knows her secret; should he tell?

The Williamsburg Years, 1780–1781

The Rebel #1

Josiah's great-grandson, Thomas Hutchinson, didn't rob the apothecary shop where he works. So why does he wind up in jail, and will he ever get out?

The Thief #2

Someone's stealing horses in Williamsburg! But is the masked rider Josiah sees the real culprit, and who's behind the mask?

The Burden #3

Thomas knows secrets he can't share. So what can he do when a crazed Walter Clark holds him at gunpoint over a secret he doesn't even know?

The Prisoner #4

As war rages in Williamsburg, Thomas' mentor refuses to fight and is carried off by the Patriots. Now which side will Thomas choose?

The Invasion #5

Word comes that Benedict Arnold and his men are ransacking plantations. Can Thomas and his family protect their homestead—even when it's invaded by British soldiers who take Caroline as a hostage?

The Battle #6

Thomas is surrounded by war! Can he tackle still another fight, taking orders from a woman he doesn't like—and being forbidden to talk about his missing brother?

The Charleston Years, 1860–1861

The Misfit #1

When the crusade to abolish slavery reaches full swing, Thomas Hutchinson's great-grandson Austin is sent to live with slave-holding relatives. How can he ever fit in?

The Ally #2

Austin resolves to teach young slave Henry-James to read, even though it's illegal. If Uncle Drayton finds out, will both boys pay the ultimate price?

The Threat #3

Trouble follows Austin to Uncle Drayton's vacation home. Who are those two men Austin hears scheming against his uncle—and why is a young man tampering with the family stagecoach?

The Trap #4

Austin's slave friend Henry-James beats hired hand Narvel in a wrestling match. Will Narvel get the revenge he seeks by picking fights and trapping Austin in a water well?

The Hostage #5

As north and south move toward civil war, Austin is kidnapped by men determined to stop his father from preaching against slavery. Can he escape?

The Escape #6

With the Civil War breaking out, Austin tries to keep Uncle Drayton from selling Henry-James at the slave auction. Will it work, and can Austin flee South Carolina with the rest of the Hutchinsons before Confederate soldiers find them?

The Chicago Years, 1928–1929

The Trick #1

Rudy and Hildy Helen Hutchinson and their father move to Chicago to live with their rich great-aunt Gussie. Can they survive the bullies they find—not to mention Little Al, a young schemer with hopes of becoming a mobster?

The Chase #2

Rudy and his family face one problem after another—including an accident that sends Rudy to the doctor, and the disappearance of Little Al. But can they make it through a deadly dispute between the mob and the Ku Klux Klan?

The Capture #3

It's Christmastime, but Rudy finds nothing to celebrate. Will his attorney father's defense of a Jewish boy accused of murder—and Hildy Helen's kidnapping—ruin far more than the holiday?

The Stunt #4

Rudy gets in trouble wing-walking on a plane. But can he stay standing as he finds himself in the middle of a battle for racial equality—and Aunt Gussie's dangerous fight for workers' rights?

Available at a Christian bookstore near you

FOCUS ON THE FAMILY®

Like this book?

Then you'll love *Clubhouse* magazine! It's written for kids just like you, and it's loaded with great stories, interesting articles, puzzles, games, and fun things for you to do. Some issues include posters, too! With your parents' permission, we'll even send you a complimentary copy.

Simply write to Focus on the Family, Colorado Springs, CO 80995 (in Canada, write P.O. 9800, Stn. Terminal, Vancouver, B.C. V6B 4G3) and mention that you saw this offer in the back of this book. Or, call 1-800-A-FAMILY (in Canada, call 1-800-661-9800).

You may also visit our Web site (www.family.org) to learn more about the ministry or find out if there is a Focus on the Family office in your country.

•   •   •

"Adventures in Odyssey" is a fantastic series of books, videos, and radio dramas that's fun for the entire family—parents, too! You'll love the twists and turns found in the novels, as well as the excitement packed into every video. And the 30 albums of radio dramas (available on audiocassette or compact disc) are great to listen to in the car, after dinner . . . even at bedtime! You can hear "Adventures in Odyssey" on the radio, too. Call Focus on the Family for a listing of local stations airing these programs or to request any of the "Adventures in Odyssey" resources. They're also available at Christian bookstores everywhere.

Focus on the Family is an organization that is dedicated to helping you and your family establish lasting, loving relationships with each other and the Lord. It's why we exist! If we can assist you or your family in any way, please feel free to contact us. We'd love to hear from you!